The Bramble Maze

The Bramble Maze

Stephen Bolger

To order additional copies of this book, contact:
Xlibris Corporation
0-800-644-6988
www.xlibrispublishing.co.uk
Orders@xlibrispublishing.co.uk
301261

Contents

The Bramble Maze

"Grandad, are you going to collect the boys anytime today?"

Grandad was standing under his prized apple tree.

"What's that, Nana?"

Nana made her way across to Grandad.

"Are you going to collect the boys? You told them you would be early."

"Yes, I am going now, it's just them crows."

Grandad pointed up to the top of the apple tree. At the top of the apple tree were thirty, maybe more, crows.

"Would you look at them? Of all the apple trees in the orchard, they have to land on this one. I would not mind if they took the apples off the ground, but no, not them. They have to take the ones from the tree."

"Would you ever leave them poor crows alone and go and collect the boys?"

"But, Nana, this tree of all trees."

"Tell you what."

"What?"

"You go and collect the boys, and I will guard the apple tree till you come back."

"You would do that for me?"

"Yes, I would, but only if you go now for the boys."

"Okay, it's a deal. I'm gone, but you have to promise to stay here till I get back and keep them crows away."

"Okay, I promise." But Grandad did not see Nana's fingers crossed behind her back.

Grandad headed across the garden, around the front of the house, down the front garden, and out the gate to his car.

"Sometimes that woman surprises me," he said out loud.

Grandad got into the car, started the engine, and drove down the dirt track on his way to collect the boys.

As soon as Nana heard Grandad's car drive away, she went straight back into the house to finish her baking.

"I have to get these done before the boys get here, or they will never forgive me."

Nana looked out the window to see twice as many crows on the tree as before. Nana tittered to herself. *Well, if there's no apples on the tree, Grandad won't spend all his time there, he will look after the other trees in the orchard.*

The Boys

The two boys were running around the house screaming and shouting at each other.

"That's my Game Boy," roared Steven. "Dad, Dad, will you speak to Louis before I kill him?"

"Mom, Steven won't leave me alone."

Paul and Anne (Steven and Louis's mom and dad) sat at the kitchen table, looking at each other.

"You know what, I am glad they are going to your mom's for a while."

"Yes, Paul, I won't know what to do with all that peace and quiet when the two of them are gone."

"Poor Mom. I don't think she knows what she is letting herself in for."

"Louis, give that game back to Steven."

"But, Dad, it's my game, mine is the red one."

"Give it back, and the two of you go to your rooms and get packed, you're going to Nana's in fifteen minutes."

The two lads scattered to their rooms.

"Have I gone deaf, Paul?"

"No, Anne, this is what it's going to be like for four weeks. You know what, we could mind them on the weekends and send them to your Mom's during the week."

"Paul, that's a good idea."

They both laughed.

"Here's your dad now."

Paul went and opened the door for Grandad.

"Hi, Paul. Hi, Anne, it's very quite here. Am I in the wrong house? Where are the boys?"

"Packing, Dad. Do you want a cup of coffee, Dad?"

"Yes, Paul, thanks."

"Hi, Grandad."

"Hello, Louis, how are you? Are you packed and ready?"

"Yes, Grandad."

"I better go and check Louis's bag, Dad. You never know what he has packed, and you know what he's like."

"Yes, Anne, I do. I think that would be a smart move."

"Hi, Grandad."

"Hello, Steve, how are you?"

"Good, Grandad, I am packed. Can we go now?"

"In a few minutes."

"Steven, let Grandad have a cup of coffee."

"Steven, come down here till I check your bag."

Steven ran back down the hall with his bag.

"Everything seems fine, no DVDs."

"No, Dad, Louis has them packed."

"Now you both listen to me, if I have to go to Grandad's because either of you caused trouble, then you will pay a dear price when I get you home. Do you understand? And, Louis, I mean it."

"Yes, Dad," both the boys answered.

"Okay, give me a hug."

Paul hugged both the kids.

"Have a good time. If you need anything, ring me."

"Okay, Dad." Both boys hugged Anne.

"See you later, Mom."

"See you later and be good."

"We will, we promise."

"Thanks, Dad, for taking the kids. Sorry you got no coffee."

"Anytime, Paul, make the best of the time. Trust me, it will go so fast."

"Do worry we will."

"Don't worry about the coffee, I will get one on the way home."

"And, Dad, please don't get them sweets, they have eaten nothing but junk since yesterday. They're so hyper, they're up since five a.m."

Grandad just smiled. "They are going on holidays, Paul."

"Right."

"So are they ready, Anne?"

"Yes, Dad."

"Right, boys, let's go."

The two boys ran to Grandad's car.

"Okay, before a fight starts about who's getting in the front, you both are getting in the back."

"But, Grandad, I am the eldest. I should be in the front."

"I know, Steven, but we have to collect Grandma on the way."

"Dad, are you collecting Mom?"

"No, Anne, I am not, but they don't know that."

Anne started laughing.

With the boys and Grandad in the car,

"Right, see you in four weeks."

"Bye, Dad." Both Paul and Anne stood at the door waving as Grandad and the boys drove out of Esker Gate, heading for Wicklow. Grandad beeped and waved.

"Right, boys, we're off to Wicklow for the holidays and to give your mom and dad a well-deserved break. So who's going to sing the first song?"

"Louis is, Grandad."

"No, I am not, I sang the last time. It's your turn."

"It's okay, boys, don't fight over who's going to sing first. I will sing the first song, now let me think."

"Ah no, Grandad, I suppose I will."

"Good man, Steven. Right, so what are you going to sing?"

"I think 'Thriller,' Grandad."

"Okay, that sounds like a good song. So off you go."

Steven started, and soon after, Louis joined in.

Very soon, the car was rocking its way to Wicklow.

Grandad laughed. He could see in the mirror Louis and Steven giving the song their best, actions and all.

"Brilliant, boys, keep it coming. Right, boys, I have to stop at that garage to get some diesel."

"Okay, Grandad, can I have a drink?"

"Yes, Louis. And, Steven, do you want one?"

"Yes, please, Grandad."

Grandad pulled into the garage and stopped at the garage doors.

"Right, you both wait here, I won't be long. What do you want to drink?"

"Can I have Coke?"

"And you, Louis?"

"I want Coke as well."

"Okay, two bottles of Coke."

Grandad got out of the car taking his keys with him and went into the garage. After a few minutes, Grandad came out of the garage carrying a bag and a cup. Grandad got back into the car.

"Right, I will give you the bag, Steven, and you share it out and don't forget to keep some for Sarah and no fighting."

"Okay, Grandad." Stephen looked into the bag.

"Wow, Grandad. Did you spend all your money?"

"Let me see."

Steven held the bag over to Louis; Louis looked into the bag.

"Wow."

Steven took out two bottles of Coke, a six-pack of Mars bars, a six-pack of Bounty bars, a six-pack of Twix, three bags of jellies, three bars of Toblerone Fruit and Nut, three bars of nougat, and a bag of mints.

"Wow, Grandad, you got a lot."

"Yes, well, enjoy them. You know there are no shops at Nana's, and Nana only goes shopping on a Saturday, so they have to last a while before you can get a chance to get to some shops."

"We don't mind, we always have Nana's apple pies."

"I suppose you do at that."

Grandad could hear the bags being ripped open.

"Hay, Grandad."

"Yes, Louis?"

"You got no diesel, and when are we collecting Nana?"

"Oh, silly me. Well, the next time we are at the garage, remind me to get some." Grandad looked down at his fuel tank. It was full.

Good job. I filled it up on the way to collect the kids. He never answered about Nana.

"Right, where were we? Oh yes, right, Steven, you were singing, and you were doing a good job, so how about some more?"

But all Grandad could hear was *munch*.

I don't think I will get any more songs out of you pair today, am I?"

Grandad started the car and made his way out of the garage, back on to the main road. He looked at his watch.

"About forty-five minutes should see us home. Steven, could you give me a few mints, please, and could you open them for me?"

"Sure, Grandad." Steven reached over and handed Grandad the bag of mints.

Grandad put the mints on the passenger seat. He took one out of the bag and popped it into his mouth and handed the bag back to Steven. "Thanks, do you know when we get home, you two can help me collect the apples from the trees. I want to try and save some before the crows get them all. They have been giving me hell this year. For some reason, there seems to be a lot of them more than any other year, and they are destroying the apples. If they keep it up, there will be no apple pies."

There was no answer from the kids. Grandad looked in the rearview mirror, the two kids had fallen asleep,

"Oh well, looks like I am on my own. They must have had an early start." Grandad continued driving. He drove all the way to the Glen of the Downs with not a move or word from the kids.

Grandad rang Nana about five minutes before he got home.

"I will be there in five, you have to come out to the car and see this."

Grandad stopped the car at the wooden fence. Nana was standing at the gate. She waved at Grandad, and he waved back.

Nana walked over to the car. Grandad pointed to the backseat.

Nana looked into the car to see Steven asleep upright with his head dropped to the right, and Louis asleep with his head dropped to the left. Both Steven's and Louis's heads were touching. Louis had a mint stuck to his forehead right in the center, and Steven had a half-eaten bar of chocolate in his hand, which had melted and was now running down his hand onto his tee-shirt and down on to his pants. Louis had a bottle of Coke in his hand. It was opened, but not a drop spilled.

"Ah, God love them, were they all right?"

"Yes, as good as gold. They were asleep nearly all the way."

The kids woke up.

"Nana."

"Come on, babies."

The lads got out of the car and went with Nana to the house.

Grandad followed on carrying the bags.

No sign of Sarah. They must be running late, he thought to himself. *Thomas said he would be here early. Ah well, I suppose they will be here when they're here.*

Sarah

Sarah woke up. She stretched in the bed, looking at the wall at the end of her bed. There was a poster of Neil Diamond, her favorite singer, and under that was a poster of the Bee Gees, her favorite group. She didn't care for the singers that were out now, well, except for Robbie Williams and Ronan Keating, she made an exception for them. To the right of the posters was a window and then a wall with a dressing unit. Running back to the door on top of the unit was a TV and a CD player with a stack of CDs and a stack of DVDs on either side of the TV. Then it hit her, today was Saturday. She was going to Gran's today for the summer holidays for four weeks, while her mom and dad went to Spain. They wanted to buy a holiday home over there.

Sarah jumped out of the bed, grabbed her housecoat, put it on while going downstairs. When she entered the kitchen, her mom, Gail, was standing at the cooker.

"Morning, hon, how are you?"

"Great, Mom, thanks."

"I am making some tea and toast, do you want some?"

"Yes, please, just tea, no toast. Thanks."

"Well, today, you're off to Nan's. I wish you would change your mind and come to Spain with Dad and me."

"Did someone call me?" Thomas, Sarah's dad, came into the kitchen. "I'll have a cup of tea, if there's one going."

Gail was making the tea.

"Well, Sarah, I wish you would rethink about going to Spain with us, it's not too late to get you a ticket."

"No thanks, Mom, there's nothing for me to do over there except sit on the beach all day, and that's boring."

"Okay, hon, I understand. Here's your tea, and yours, Tom."

"Did I ask you if you want toast, Sarah?"

"Yes, Mom, and no thanks, just tea. Mom, I am going up to start packing."

"Okay, hon, don't forget the things I got you yesterday. They're in a bag in the front room, and I got you that book you wanted."

"Ah, thanks, Mom." Sarah took her tea and went into the front room and got the bag, and then she went back upstairs.

When Sarah left the kitchen, Gail said to Tom, "What are we going to do? I wish you would say something."

"About what?"

"About Sarah, she should be spending her summer holidays with us."

"Ah, don't worry, she will be grand down in your mother's. I might even stay there myself."

"Don't you start."

"Look, Gail, if she wants to spend her summer holidays down in your mother's, well then, let her. She will be okay there. Anyway, the boys will be there, and you know how she gets on with them, and we are going to be running to and from properties and selling agencies. I don't think it would be much of a holiday for her."

"I suppose you're right."

Thomas finished his tea. "You know I am."

18

"Right, I will give her a shout and see if she is ready, and I will drop by the bank on the way home. Sure you don't want to come?"

"I would love to, but I have to sort the flight tickets out and start packing. Don't forget to tell Mom I said hello, and I will see her when we get back. Oh, tell her I will ring her tonight and ask her for the small blue case. She will know the one."

"Okay, I will ask her."

"Sarah, Sarah," Dad called upstairs, "are you ready?"

"Yes, Dad, I will be down in a minute. I am just putting my hair up."

"Okay, try not to be too long, I have a lot to do after I drop you at Nan's."

"Is she ready?" asked Gail.

"She will be down in a second. She is just putting her hair up."

"Here, Dad." Sarah tossed her bag down the stairs to her dad. "I will be down in a second."

Thomas went out to the car, putting Sarah's bag into the car on the backseat. Looking into the car, he said to himself, *I must clean this car. I wish that child would hurry up, or I will be late for the bank.*

Sarah came down the stairs.

"Right, Mom, I'm ready."

"Okay, give me a hug." Hugging Sarah, her mom asked, "Have you got everything? Do you need anything?"

"No thanks, Mom, I have everything. You have a good holiday."

Gail hugged Sarah once more. "And be good to Grandma."

"I will."

With that, Sarah was standing behind her dad. "Okay, Dad, I am ready."

"Right, let's go." Dad and Sarah got into the car. "You have everything?"

"Yes, Dad."

"Okay, let's go." Dad drove out of the estate and up to the north road and then on to the M50, heading for the N11.

Sarah sat in the front seat, delighted that today had come. She was heading down to her grandmother's for four weeks of her summer holidays."

"I am stopping at the garage for petrol. Do you want anything in the garage while I am in there?"

"No, thanks."

Thomas got out of the car to get petrol. When he came back, he handed Sarah a bag with 7UP, sweets, and some chocolates.

Sarah looked at the bag and then looked at her dad. "Thanks, Dad."

From under his coat, he pulled out a small furry toy.

"Here," he said, "that's the last one in the collection."

Sarah gave her dad a big hug. "Thanks, Dad."

"Put your seatbelt back on so we can go."

"Yes, Dad." Sarah put the seatbelt back on.

Sarah looked out the window and across at the forest, she loved the freedom and quietness at Gran's.

No one to nag her about her hair or what to wear.

Mom said she was too skinny.

"Me skinny? Not a hope. I am nine years of age, four foot seven inches tall, and five stone six pounds. That's not skinny, that's just nice." Sarah's skin was tan and her hair a mousy brown.

"Okay, ready?" said Dad.

"Yes," said Sarah, "thanks, Dad."

Dad drove out of the garage and on down the N11.

"I wonder, will Steven and Louis be in Gran's when I get there?"

Sarah loved it when Steven and Louis, her cousins, were at Gran's. Steven and Louis are brothers. Steven is eleven, and Louis is ten, but both of them are like chalk and cheese.

Steven is quite a deep thinker, who loves to take things apart and put them back together just to see how they work, but Louis just loves to take things apart and walk away, leaving them in a mess. Louis is the sort of kid who would head-butt a tree because he can. He is never wrong and very strong-willed.

Steven may be relaxed and laid back, but don't dare cross him.

He can have a nasty temper when annoyed, but lucky that's not often. Whereas Louis would fight with you one minute, and the next, he'd be your best friend.

Thomas turned off the N11 and onto a small road.

"Not long now till we reach Grandma's." Sarah looked to the side window of the car. They were starting to drive uphill. She knew this because she could look down on the N11. There were trees everywhere, and she could see back to Wicklow bay. Dad turned again to the left and across a dirt track after a few minutes. There was a wooden fence across the track with a gate.

"Right," said Thomas, getting out of the car to open the gate, "we're here."

"I am going to walk up to the house," said Sarah. Dad did not answer; he just nodded.

Sarah started walking; it was only five hundred feet to the gate in the stone wall around Grandma's house. Beyond the gate was Grandma's house; it was an old cottage when Grandma and Grandad and Angela bought it. That was before Sarah was born. When they built it, they put on a downstairs toilet and a sitting room and extended the kitchen. They also added four bedrooms upstairs and a sunroom. From there, you could see all the gardens. They turned it from a two-bedroom cottage to a six-bedroom cottage out the back, and to the sides of the house, they had gardens like nothing you ever seen before. This was thanks to Angela, there was all sorts of plants, trees, and shrubs in full bloom and so full of life.

Angela is Grandma's twin sister. She looked after the gardens; she had hands of magic when it came to planting. Angela loved to sit over coffee and chat; but most of the time, she liked to be on her own in the gardens, except for family. Angela said she preferred her gardens over people. She would say you can work with plants, but people are something else. No, give her plants and trees any day, they don't answer you back. Sarah remembered her mom telling her that there were killings for weeks over the name of the house. Nana wanted one name, and Angela wanted another. Grandad stayed out of the agreement.

In the end, Grandad won.

"Why not leave the name as it is, the Glen? After all, the name has been on the house since the year dot, and it's known to everyone as the Glen, and if you look around, it's a name that suits, not names such as the Cedars or the Elms. There are names that don't suit this house, where the Glen seems to suit the house. I don't know, girls, it's up to you. That's just my penny's worth."

And the name stayed.

The Glen

"Hey, Sarah," Grandma said.

Sarah ran to Grandma, hugging her. "Hi, Nan."

"My, don't you look well today."

"Thank you, Nan."

"Well, why don't you go on into the house? Steven and Louis are inside. And get yourself some apple tart, that's if Louis hasn't eaten it all."

"Okay, thanks, Nan."

Sarah headed into the house.

Gran went to Sarah's dad. "Do you need a hand?"

"No thanks, Gran, it's only one bag, and it's light for a change."

"Sure, I will drop it into the house."

"Okay, Thomas, I will go in and put on the kettle."

Sarah went into the kitchen. "Hi," she said to Louis and Steven.

"Hi," they both answered together.

"Want some apple tart?" asked Steven.

"Yes, please," answered Sarah.

Steven looked at the plate; there was only one slice left. He looked at Louis. "You're unbelievable," said Steven.

"What?" asked Louis. Steven just shook his head.

Looking at the table, there was a jug of orange juice and a jug of milk.

"Can I have some milk?"

"Sure," said Steven.

"I will get that for you," said Grandad.

They did not see Grandad come in the back door.

"Hi, Grandad," all three said together.

"Hay, gang."

Sarah came over and hugged her Grandad.

"How was your trip?" asked Grandad.

"Oh, it was okay."

"How is mom and dad?"

"We are both great," said Thomas as he came in the kitchen door with Grandma.

"Good," said Grandad.

"Tea or coffee?" asked Grandma, walking into the kitchen with Thomas.

"Coffee would be good. Oh, before I forget, can we borrow the small case from you, the blue one?"

"Sure, Thomas, I will get it for you as soon as we have our coffee."

"Can we go, please?" asked Steven.

"Yes," said Grandad, "but don't go far."

"Okay," said Steven, "we won't."

Steven looked at Louis and Sarah.

"Don't forget to ring home and let us know how you are," said Thomas to Sarah.

"We are leaving at six p.m. tomorrow evening."

"I will, I mean, I won't. You know what I mean, Dad."

Thomas just nodded.

All three got up together and went out the back.

Sarah grabbed her bag on the way out.

Outside, Steven said, "Why don't we go down to the camp for a while? Your dad is going to be chatting to Grandad and Grandma for ages."

Sarah and Louis agreed. "Okay, but only for a while."

"Okay, Sarah, let's go."

The three of them headed out the back gate and down toward the river. They had to climb over a fence halfway down to the river and across the river, crossing over the little bridge and into the forest.

The farther they went into the forest, the darker it got.

"How long are you staying?" Sarah asked the two boys.

"Four weeks," said Steven. "And what about you, Sarah?"

"Oh, four weeks, maybe a little longer, depends."

"Depends on what?" asked Steven.

"On Mom."

"Why your mom?"

"Mom and Dad are going to Spain, they want to buy a villa there, so they think they will be four weeks. But it could be longer."

"Oh, okay, I understand, I think."

They came to a clearing in the forest. Behind them, in front of them, and to the left were trees, but to the right was a ten-foot wall of brambles. They walked along the brambles for fifty or sixty feet till they came to a gap. Being careful, they went into the gap, leading them into a maze. Following the trail in the maze, it brought them to a clearing in the brambles.

This is where their camp is.

"Okay, we are here." This was their secret camp.

"Will I light the fire?" said Louis, taking a lighter from his pocket.

"Okay," said Sarah, kneeling on the ground. She opened her bag. She reached into the bag and took out three bottles of water and a packet of biscuits, a bottle of 7UP, some sweets, and some chocolates and a furry toy.

"Nice one," said Louis.

"If somebody didn't eat everything in the car on the way here, we would have had some goodies ourselves."

"Not to worry, there's plenty here for everybody, and you can't blame Louis for been hungry."

"Thanks," said Louis. "And Steven ate more than his share as well, but as usual, I get the blame for everything."

"Don't worry, there's plenty here for everybody," said Sarah.

"Well, there won't be if Steven gets his hands on them. Mom says he has a lapse of food memory.

The more he eats, the less he remembers, and do you know what, Sarah? Ask him where the chocolate cake vanished to on Sunday. Looks like it melted in the fridge, even Dad was amazed."

"Yes, Louis, and don't forget to tell Sarah what Mom found under your bed last week. Go on, I dare you to tell her."

"I don't need to 'cause there was nothing under my bed. That was put there by me. Seems Mom found your stash under my bed. Clever Steven, you knew that I would get the blame. Anyway, we all know that you're the only one that eats the minichocolate swiss rolls, and what did Mom find? Wrappers of them, not just one wrapper but dozens of them."

"You should give Steven a break, Louis."

"Yeah right," said Louis, "that works both ways. Seems Steven is always ready to blame me, but he is never ready to take the blame when he is wrong. Oh no, blame Louis, it's the easy way out for him."

"I have never seen two brothers disagree with each other as much as you two do. You two are unbelievable, and I don't need to hear all this, I want to just enjoy this holiday and have fun. Now, Louis, you should say sorry to Steven."

"Ah, Sarah, you're starting to sound like my Mom."

"Okay, Louis, I won't say another word for the rest of this holiday."

"I didn't mean that."

"It's okay, Louis, I know what you meant."

"See, Louis, you always manage to upset everybody."

"It's okay, Steven, let's just leave it."

"Okay, Sarah, sorry. Louis, say you're sorry."

Louis never answered; he just carried on lighting the fire.

The Brambles

The kids were tired. They had spent the last three hours playing and planning their battle with forces from an unknown land. The three kids—Steve, Louis, and Sarah—had played this game in the brambles every Saturday for the last four months. Each time, they would take turns being the leader. Except the time Sarah could not come to Nana's because she had a chest infection.

Happy with their day's adventure, they sat around their little fire discussing their day's events.

They finished up their day this way every Saturday that they were here before going home to their grandmother's.

"Did you see the way I fought with them?" said Steven. "There must have being fifty of them."

"Yes," said Louis. "If it weren't for me coming in from behind, you would have being killed, you were outnumbered by at least twenty to one. You did not stand a chance."

"No, he was not," said Sarah. "Last week, Steven helped you out when you were trapped in the bramble with no way out, he never thought of himself, he just charged in, you were lucky."

"Right, it's time we started to head home. Grandma will be worried about us, it's starting to get late."

"Okay," they all agreed.

Louis jumped up and grabbed the bottle of water, pouring it over the fire to put the fire out.

"Hay, why don't we come down early on tomorrow?"

"Don't be a fool," said Sarah. "You know Grandma won't let us go on Sunday till we have our chores done, and Sunday is a family day."

"Yes," said Louis, "but if we talk to Grandad, you know what he's like. He can get around Grandma and ask her to let us go early."

"Okay," said Steven, "it's worth a try."

"Right so," said Sarah, "that's what we will do."

Sarah jumped up and pushed Louis, who was standing with his back to Sarah.

"Hay, what's that for?"

"You know," said Sarah.

"No, I don't," said Louis.

"Yes, you do," said Sarah.

"You stuck something on to my leg."

"No, I did not."

"Yes, you did."

"No, I did not."

"Okay," said Steven.

"It's not okay," said Sarah. "It hurt, and it wasn't nice."

"But I did not do anything, I had my back to you, so how could I stick anything into your leg?" said Louis.

"Well, someone did," said Sarah, "and Steven was over there, so who does that leave? The fairies?"

"Well, not me. I had my back to you putting out the fire."

While Sarah and Louis were nose to nose, they heard Steven cry out. They both turned toward Steven, who was lying on the ground.

"Okay, who tripped me?"

Both Louis and Sarah looked at each other.

"But you're over there, you must have caught your foot in something."

"I did not, I was tripped and pushed."

"Well, if we are over here, and you're over there, who tripped you?" They all looked at each other.

"And who stuck you?" said Steven.

"I know," said, Steven. "It's you pair up to your tricks again. Well, you can both do as you wish, I'm off home."

Steven made his way toward the gap in the bramble bush when all of a sudden, he went flying headfirst into the bushes.

Before he knew anything, he was caught in the thorns.

Louis and Sarah ran over to Steven and were beside him in seconds, pulling him from the bush.

"Ahh, what did you do that for?"

"I'm stuck, and all the thorns are everywhere."

Louis pulled at Steven, getting him back on his feet. At the same time, Sarah was trying to get the thorns out of Steven's jumper.

"Stand still," said Sarah to Steven. "You're like a big baby."

"I am not, I have thorns stuck everywhere. Look, my jumper is all ripped, and my hands and arms are cut to bits. I don't think that was very funny."

Sarah looked at Louis and shrugged her shoulders.

"What's the point? You can't talk to him. I am out of here."

Sarah headed through the gap in the bramble followed by Louis. They did not wait for Steven.

Steven, seeing them go, and after pulling a few more thorns from his jumper, ran to catch up with Louis and Sarah.

None of the kids spoke to each other as they headed for home, going through the bramble maze and out through the forest to the open meadows, down across the field to the river.

Louis decided to use the stepping-stones that were across the river.

"What's he doing?" asked Steven.

"I don't know," said Sarah,

"Why can't he use the bridge like the rest of us?"

Louis jumped onto the first stone, second stone, third stone, then a wobble, then splash. Louis ended bum first in the water, and he fell backward, getting soaked from head to toe.

Luckily, the water was only ten inches deep at this end."

Sarah just shook her head.

Steven wanted to laugh but did not.

Louis sat there for a few seconds. When he got up, there was water everywhere. He was soaked to the skin; he just looked at Sarah and Steven and stormed off, heading for Grandma's.

"He does that every time. Would you think that after the first six or seven times he would know he is going to end up in the water? He should have learned by now to use the bridge like the rest of us. Maybe someday, Sarah, notice I said maybe."

"Leave him be," said Sarah. "Yes, maybe someday he will learn, but I don't think it's going to be someday soon."

Steven tittered. Sarah could not hold back any longer, she burst out laughing. That edged Steven on till he started to laugh out loud.

Louis heard them laughing. He stopped and turned back facing Steven and Sarah.

"It's not funny." Louis was annoyed. Both Steven and Sarah could see this by the color on Louis's face changed to a bright red.

His temper was rising, and he was grinding his teeth.

They both stopped laughing together.

Louis turned and carried on his way.

Both Sarah and Steven said nothing; they just both looked at each other and shrugged their shoulders. In a case like this, the best thing to say was nothing. When Louis was on the verge, it did not take much to push him over; and once he was over the edge, he was uncontrollable. But he still looked very funny standing in the river with water running off him, soaked to the skin, and with a confused look on his face. *If I only had a camera, the picture would be priceless*, Sarah thought to herself. *If only.*

Grandad and Grandma

As the kids came to the last hill, heading down to Gran's, they could see Grandad in the garden looking up at the apple tree and scratching his head. He was shouting at some crows up in the tree and shaking a fist at them.

"Someday, I will get the lot of you. Eat my apples, well, we will see for how long. You wait, you dirty bunch of apple robbers, just wait." The crows paid no heed to him; they just keep on eating the apples. Sarah was the first to laugh. She started with a titter, and it exploded into an all-out explosion of laughter. After a few seconds, Louis joined in and then Steven. Grandad looked up; he could hear the kids laughing from where he was.

"What in the name of God has got into them?"

Grandma was now standing at the door of the house.

"What's wrong?"

"Nothing," said Grandad. "It's just them kids, they must be having a funny hour again."

The kids seemed to have forgotten all about their day's events and were back to their normal selves till Grandma said, "Steven, what happened to your jumper? And look at your hands."

With that, Grandma saw the state of Louis.

"What in the name of God happened to you? You're soaked to the bone."

"Fell in the stream again, Grandma. I was doing great, and when I got out to the middle of the stream, someone pushed me."

"Like all the times before, Louis."

"But, Nana—"

"No buts, Louis."

"Again," said Grandad, "in the river. How many times do you have to fall into the river before you understand there's a bridge?"

Louis just shrugged his shoulders and said, "About twelve."

This started Steven and Sarah off again.

"Get inside and clean yourself up," said Grandma.

The kids went inside and up to their rooms. By the time they were clean, Grandma was shouting for them to come for tea.

Over tea, the kids told their story of their day's events, including the issues at the end of the day, to Grandma and Grandad.

Grandad scratched his head. "You forgot the bit about the river."

"I don't think you lot should be going back up there for a while. Seems to be something odd going on up there, and I have heard stories from the locals about that maze," said Grandma.

The kids looked at each other and said nothing.

The kids were on summer holidays and were staying in their grandparents for four weeks, and this had been their first day. They had plenty of time to butter up Grandad, to get around Nana, to let them go back up to the brambles.

After tea they went into the garden and just lazed around. Still none of them spoke about what happened earlier. But all three agreed plans for tomorrow. Feeling tired and worn-out, they all had an early night as the grandparents were heading to Dublin early the next morning, and the kids would only have Angela to look after them.

But she was okay, she would spend the day in the garden, or read a book. She kind of keeps to herself most of the time. She is like that ever since she was about nine. They never found out why, and she won't tell them she preferred plants over people. The kids had their plans made for the next day, and they had spent some of their time earlier in the garden, making up these plans for most of tomorrow. They had planned a full-day fun in the maze; there were a lot of things they wanted to do, and the little issue of their grandparents going to Dublin was not going to stop them having their day's fun. Being tired, they all decided to head up to bed and got a good rest.

They all said good night to Nana, Grandad, and Annie.

The next morning, Sarah woke up. She could hear noises coming from downstairs. She started to stretch,

"Ahaaaaa, it's Sunday." Remembering that the grandparents would be gone for a while today, she was out of the bed in a flash. She grabbed her tracksuit, put it on quickly. She headed down to the kitchen. Something smelled good; Grandma was in the kitchen. "Morning, Sarah, breakfast is ready for you and the other two. Do you want to go and call them for me please?"

"Yes, Gran."

Sarah called up the stairs, "STEVEN, LOUIS, breakfast."

Sarah went back into the kitchen.

"Hmm." It smelled good.

"You know that we have to go to Dublin today, we won't be long, a couple of hours, at most five hours. Well, I hope it won't be that long, and we will be back before you finish breakfast. And, Sarah, keep an eye on them, you know what that pair is like when they're on their own. They can be a handful. I have left everything ready, so there's nothing for you or the others to do till I get back except enjoy the sunshine." Grandma got her coat and bag.

"Everything is ready, make sure the boys eat their breakfast. Will you be okay till I get back?"

"Yes, we will be, Nana. Now don't worry, I will look after things till you get back, now go on."

"Thanks, Sarah, I knew I could trust you."

"Okay, and Annie is out back. Call her in for breakfast please."

"Okay, Gran, now stop fussing and go. We will be, Grand."

Gran kissed Sarah on the forehead and was gone out the door.

Grandad was all ready in the car; he waved at Sarah and blew a kiss to her. It was something Grandad always did since as far back as she could remember.

Sarah caught the kiss in her hand and blew one back to Grandad. Grandad grabbed the kiss and put his hand over his mouth then waved back at Sarah; then they drove down the drive and were gone, on their way to Dublin.

Sarah ran back up the stairs, calling Steven and Louis as she ran. She was shouting, "Get up, get up! Come on!"

She ran inside Steven's room, and with one bounce, she landed upright and standing on Steven's bed.

"Get up, come on."

Steven screamed at Sarah, "Get out! I'm up!" as Sarah jumped off the bed.

Louis arrived at Steven's bedroom door.

"Where's the fire?"

"Ah, come on, breakfast is ready. The sooner we eat it, the sooner we can go to the brambles."

They all went downstairs and sat at the table.

They wolfed down their food; they were all eager to get out to the brambles. This is the first day of their holidays, and they wanted to make the most of it.

"You're a pig, Louis," said Steven. "Snort, snort."

Sarah laughed.

"Don't encourage him, or he will get worse."

"Sorry." But she still giggled.

All three were washed, fed, and on their way in twenty minutes. It was now 10:30 a.m., and they had a twenty-minute walk to their camp. The usual banter went on, on the way to the brambles, pushing, shoving.

"Oh, I won't need any help from you today," said Steven to Louis.

"We will see about that. You did not need my help last week, did you? And you were nearly killed and the time before that as well."

"Well, I am ready today. What do you think, Sarah?"

There was no answer from her, and the boys looked back at Sarah. She was already in a world of her own.

As they came to the gap in the brambles, Sarah was still in her own world.

"Come on, Sarah," said Steven, "we're here." They went through the gap and made their way through the maze to their camp.

"I wonder where that leads to," said Louis, pointing at the left turn in the hedgerow bending of to the left. "We have never went down there."

"Well, I don't know," said Steven.

"Well, let's look," said Louis. Sarah still seemed to be in dreamland.

"Okay," said Steven. "Come on, Sarah."

"What? Where are we going?"

"We're going to see what's down here."

"Down where?"

"Here, to the left."

"Oh well, okay." The boys headed off with Sarah tagging behind.

"Well, left or right?" said Steven to Louis.

"Left," Louis said when they came to the next split in the maze.

At the next split, Louis called for Sarah to catch up.

Steven said, "Right."

At the next split, Louis said, "Okay." On they went left.

When they came to the next split, Louis said, "Left or right? Which way do you want to go, Sarah?"

Louis turned. "Where has she gone?"

"I don't know," said Steven. "She was right behind us."

Louis called out, "SARAH, SARAH! Ah, come on, where are you?"

"Come on," said Steven.

"What?" said Louis.

"We have to go back to see where she is."

"She spoils everything. Girls."

"Ah, shut up. If you got lost, she would be the first to look for you. Now come on." They retraced their steps back to the camp. There was no sign of Sarah.

"Where's she gone?"

"Probably gone home. She was a bit off. Well, let's go, Louis."

"Where?" said Louis.

"To check back the way we came," said Steven. "And then if we have to, we will go back to Nan's to see if she is there." Off the two boys headed in the direction of Nan's, retracing their steps the way they came and back toward Grandma's, all the time calling Sarah's name but with no answer.

When they got back to Grandma's, there was no sign of Sarah anywhere.

"What now, Steven?"

"We will have to go back to the maze."

"Why?" asked Louis.

"Well, maybe she fell and was knocked out, I don't know. But we have to find her before Grandma and Grandad get home."

"Where did you see her last?" asked Steven.

"I'm not sure, I think after the left, left, and right, I think."

"Okay," said Steven, "we will go back to the camp in the maze and start from there. We will check every turn left and right just in case she took a wrong turn, and she can't hear us calling out."

"Do you know how long that will take?" said Louis.

"I don't care, we will just do it till we find her," said Steven.

"I don't think she is lost, I think she is just hiding. She is doing it to get back at us over yesterday."

"That's being silly. You know Sarah is not like that."

"Well, why else would she have gone back to Nan's without telling us?" Steven never answered Louis; he was feeling very guilty. He is the oldest, and he should have made sure to keep them together.

But he did not, and now it was up to him to find out where Sarah was. If it's the last thing he will ever do, he will find her; and from now on, he will make sure they always stay together no matter what.

He would have to find her before Grandma got home, and that won't be long.

The boys went back to the camp in the maze.

"Do you think we should go back to the house and tell Annie that we can't find Sarah?" said Louis.

"No, not yet. We haven't looked everywhere. Wait till we check everywhere, and then if we can't find her, we will go back to Nan's and tell Annie. You know Annie, she would explode, and we will never hear the end of it."

Annie is Grandma's twin sister. She is great fun to be with, but she is a quiet sort of person. You would never know she was around except when something went wrong. Then look out as all hell would break loose but would only be for a short while; then she would be sorry.

But most of the time, you would not know Annie was around.

You would never hear her or see her; she was like a ghost. That is unless you stood on one of her plants or did something wrong to her. Then you would be the worst in the world, and you would have no manners, and Annie did not mince her words with you. When she started, she let you have both barrels, and she did not care who was around or who you were or who she offended; but later when things calmed down, Annie would get upset for what she had said or done, and she would spend all day saying she was sorry. Nana said that Annie would shout before she would think. But no matter what, the three kids loved Annie.

She would make a fuss over them when they were sick or stand by them when they were wrong. She was the only one who could give out to them, and they would not sulk. Many a falling out she had with the kids' parents over them giving out to the kids for something they done wrong, but when she got you on your own, she would give you a roasting, the fire-and-brimstone lecture. But after she was finished, she would give you a hug that would leave you breathless.

The kids were well used to her by now, that was just their Annie, and they were the only ones who were allowed to call Angela Annie.

Mogieland

Sarah was walking behind the two lads. She slowed down a little; she thought someone was following them. She stayed up with the lads up to the brambles, but as they entered the bramble, she now thought she could hear a voice. The voice seemed to be following them. She thought she was losing her mind; she could now hear a voice and see movement in the bramble. No point in saying anything to the lads 'cause they would only laugh at her, so she just followed them. When they got to a turn, the lads were going right. But up about ten feet was a second right turn; then she saw him, it, whatever it was. It was fast and small, but she saw it move, not run, through a gap in the bramble.

Got you, she said to herself; she went after it. The gap was very small. She squeezed through on her belly, just about making it before she got back to her feet. She saw it disappear through a small opening in the bramble on the far side of the clearing. *I knew I was not going mad.* She did not get a good look at whatever it was, but she knew it was there. Sarah headed across the clearing to the small opening in the bramble. This was grand; she could go through this opening on her hands and knees. As she went into the opening, things started to get dark and cold, and the farther she went, the darker and colder it got. At last, she came to the end of the opening; she stood shocked at what she saw. There was no color, and everything was black or gray. The trees, the grass, the hedges, the sky, everything. After a few seconds, she saw something she did not know what. It was about half her size, and she was four feet seven inches. It was covered in wrinkles with sad big blue eyes and was shaped like a funny-shaped ball with an out-of-place face and stumpy legs and an odd-shaped head. It stood looking at Sarah. Neither of them moved; they both just looked at each other. After what seemed like ages, Sarah was the first to speak.

Sarah said, "Hello, what's your name, and where am I?" There was no answer from this, whatever it was.

Sarah thought to herself, *I'm talking to a whatever-it-is*, looking past the thing into the distance. *That's funny*, she thought to herself. A field in the distance was green, but she could see it slowly turn black as if someone was robbing the color from it.

"Oh, that's odd," she said out loud, not realizing she had said it.

The funny-looking thing walked over to Sarah and handed her a shiny small stone.

Sarah took the stone from the funny little man.

"Now you should be able to understand me. Quick, quick," said this thing, "quick before it's too late. You have to come with me." It grabbed her hand with his stumpy hand.

"We have to go." It pulled Sarah along.

"Slow down!" shouted Sarah.

"No time, we have to hurry and be quiet. They can hear, smell, and see everything." It pulled Sarah behind some dead trees. Before it stopped, he looked all around.

"It's okay here for a while but not long."

Sarah looked at this molelike thing.

"Okay, who are you? What are you? And who are they, and what are they, and where is this place, and why is everything black, and what can smell and hear everything?"

The mole thing looked at Sarah.

"You don't know?"

"No, I don't know where I am. I followed you, so how would I know?"

"Well, this is Mogieland. They are the Takers, and I am Taz. I am an Earth Keeper."

"Okay, Taz, I am Sarah, and what's going on here?"

"This land is divided in five: to the north is the Takers, next is the black forest, then there's the swamplands where the wise man lives, then the blue forest, then the Earth Keepers' lands. The Takers have found a way across the swamplands and have invaded our land and destroyed everything. Any more than that, you will have to wait till you meet Tazmaz, our leader. That's if we ever make it back to our village. The Takers are everywhere."

"Takers, what or who are they?"

"You will have to wait. Now come on, we have to go."

They ran across black fields with black trees, black hedging—not burned or anything, just black. The only thing that had color was the stream they had crossed.

"Not far now," said Taz.

They ran into a forest, a black forest. After about twenty minutes, they came to a clearing at the edge of the forest. Sarah's lungs were bursting for air; it was hard to keep up with this Earth Keeper thing.

To the right, the black forest continued. To the left, there were two mountains, one was big and the other was a lot smaller.

Taz ran toward the smaller of the two mountains, dragging Sarah along. As they got closer, they veered off to the small mountain.

Sarah could see caves dotted along the base of the small mountain.

The mountain to the right, it had a waterfall running down the middle of it.

The water was silver? No, it was blue? No, it seemed to have lots of colors. She never saw anything like that before.

And Sarah was sure she could smell the water.

That's odd, Sarah thought to herself. *A smell of water. Water does not smell. Water never smelled unless you're in a swimming pool.*

"We are here," said Taz. They went into the biggest cave; it was well lit with burning torches along the walls and light coming from things like diamonds stuck in the walls.

In the center, there was a fire and along the wall were straw and a big table full of fruits and straw all over the floors.

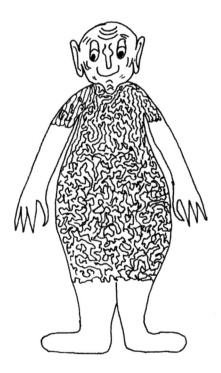

Other than the creatures that lived there, the cave was empty.

"Welcome to our home," said Taz.

"Do you all live here?" asked Sarah.

"No, just this work clan. Each clan has their own cave. There is ninety, here, and we have seventy clans throughout our lands. We all work for the Takers," Taz was talking.

Sarah could see a full-sized thing, the same as Taz only three times his size, come in the cave entrance. Now Sarah felt scared.

Taz turned to where Sarah was looking.

"Ah, this is Tazmaz, our leader. He rules over all the clans of the Earth Keepers."

Sarah looked; Tazmaz had green eyes—bright green—and a friendly face. As he approached the fire, more smaller things came from the shadows. They all looked the same, except for their eyes. Some had blue, like Taz's, the others had light blue eyes.

Sarah asked, "Taz, what was the story with the eyes?"

Taz explained that the leader had green eyes, the males had dark blue eyes, and the females, who were smaller than the males, had light blue eyes, and the young ones had yellow eyes, which change when they reach the twenty-fifth cycle, and they became male or female.

"Oh, okay," said Sarah.

The big one, Tazmaz, approached Sarah.

"Who are you?" he asked.

"Me?" said Sarah.

"Yes, you," said Tazmaz.

"I am Sarah, and who are you?"

"Well, Sarah, I am Tazmaz, leader of the Earth Keepers. Where are you from, and what do you want here in my land?"

"I am from Dublin, and I don't want anything from you or anybody."

"Then why are you here?" asked Tazmaz.

"I was in the brambles with my cousins. We are all down in my Gran's for the summer. We went to the brambles to have some fun, and then I saw him, and I followed him"—she pointed at Taz—"through the bramble maze, and here I am."

Tazmaz looked at Taz. "You know it's forbidden to enter the maze."

"Yes," said Taz. "But I got this pulling from a pouch, a drum of salt."

All the others stepped back when they saw the salt.

Salt was the only thing that the Takers had a fear of. Once it got into their system, it caused them to swell up and get sores. These sores would bleed and not heal and not stop bleeding till they ran out of blood and died. It was a painful and slow death for them; it also had the same effect on the Earth Keepers.

"Give that to Sarah," said Tazmaz to Taz. "And don't get any on you. You know how dangerous that is."

Taz handed over the drum of salt to Sarah.

"Of all the Earth Keepers, Taz, you should know better than to go into the outside world, and it is forbidden to remove anything from there.

But that still did not give you permission to go through the maze.

If you had been caught by the Takers, you know the price you would have had to pay. It would not have been worth the risk, and you would have let the Takers know that there was a way to the outside world."

"Yes, Tazmaz," said Taz. "I won't do it again."

Tazmaz looked at Sarah. "What are we going to do with you? We can't put you back in the maze for a full twenty-five cycles, and then only with the help of the gatekeeper. And with the Takers everywhere, that's going to be hard to do. Even after the twenty-five cycles have passed, it's still too dangerous. You can stay here until we can get you back to the lands where you're supposed to be. You can't go outside. You must stay in the here in our home until it's safe for you to go back to the brambles. Taz will stay here with you and keep you company. Seeing as he is the one responsible for bringing you here in the first place."

Tazmaz gave a stern look at Taz.

"And I will deal with you later for leaving our lands and crossing over through the gateway without the gatekeepers' permission to their land. You know you need to ask for permission first, and I will have to explain to the wise man why you went to the outside and why I gave you permission. I will be the one who will be held responsible at the end, and of all things to take from the outside, you took salt, and you were seen, and now we have another problem." Tazmaz just shook his head.

"I can go on all day, but what's the point? What's done is done, but you still will have to pay for breaking the rules. It's now up to you to return this Sarah back to where she belongs and with no help from any of your clan or any other Earth Keeper."

Taz was looking at the ground. "Yes, Tazmaz."

Sarah did not know where to look. She felt embarrassed for Taz.

He was only trying to help.

"Anyway, I have more important things on my mind. I can't wait for twenty-five whatevers to get home. I have to get home now."

"Well, you will have to wait for now. There is nothing we can do for now. You both are very lucky you got from the gateway to here and not being seen by the Takers. Son, don't push your luck trying to get back. If you get caught by the Takers, it's us who will have to pay the price, and that will be with our lives. I don't think you would want that to happen, so please stay where you are till it's safe for you to return to your own land."

Sarah looked at Taz.

Taz was still looking at the ground.

"Can you not bring me back to the bramble, Taz?"

"No, he can't. We have to wait till it's safe, he will not move from this cave without my permission. He is in enough trouble as it is, he does not need to get into anymore. I hope you understand what I am saying to you, Taz, and I hope for your sake you are taking it all in, and I hope you understand what I am saying, Sarah. If anything was to happen to you while you are here, the wise man would blame all of us, and we, and when I say we, I mean all the people of Mogieland, would have to answer to the wise man and the caretaker. And if our answer wasn't good enough, they would release the Tallis, and that's one thing we don't want to happen now, do we, Taz?"

Taz was still looking at the ground.

And Sarah did not know where to look.

"Yes, I think I understand, so it looks like I have to stay. But, Tazmaz, what are these things you call the Tallis?"

"You don't need to know, Sarah. All you need to know is that we must keep you safe and return you to your land."

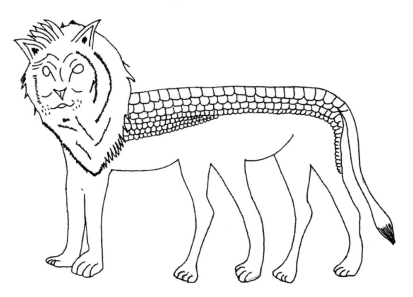

The Work Call

"But I have to get home soon before Grandma gets home, or I will be in big trouble."

Before Tazmaz could answer, there was a piercing noise. The sound it seemed to be everywhere.

Sarah put her hands over her ears.

"What's that?" she asked.

All the males looked at Tazmaz then turned and headed out of the cave, except Taz, who had to stay with Sarah.

Sarah started to follow when one of the Earth Keepers with the light blue eyes caught her by the jacket.

"It's not safe out there for you, you will have to stay here with us till the males come back."

"Why?" asked Sarah. With that, the sound stopped.

"It's the Takers calling for the workers. They will be back later. Come eat, you have to be patient and wait."

Sarah saw the apples, berries, and other fruits beside the fire, so she sat at the fire and ate some fruits.

"This is good." Sarah lay back after she had eaten; she did not remember falling asleep.

But when she woke, the cave was empty. She looked around the cave. *Where's everyone gone?* she said to herself; then she remembered they had to go to work.

Before she could answer herself, the males started to come back into the cave; they all sat around the fire and started to eat. No one spoke.

When they had finished eating, Tazmaz looked at Sarah.

"I was in your world once a long time ago when our land was the same as yours, fresh and green and full of life. That was long before the Takers came to our lands."

"Who are the Takers, and why are they here?" asked Sarah.

"The Takers are evil, they live to the north, past the swamp and the black forest. They were held in their own land by the five thorns, but one of the thorns is missing, and this broke the spell that held them in their lands. With the spell broken, this allowed the Takers to leave their land. And go wherever they pleased. They live on life, they suck the life out of all living things for nourishment. They don't eat like us. We are the Earth Keepers. We plant and give life to all plants, fruit, berries, and this is what we live on. Now the Takers have us bringing back life to the land so they can suck it dry again. If we put up any fight at all, they take the life from us, so we have to do as we are told. We are no match for them."

"I saw a field turn from green to gray when I got here. Was that the Takers?"

"Yes, that's what they do, take the life from all that's living."

"Where is the missing thorn?" asked Sarah.

"We don't know, said it's been missing ever since the last stranger came here a long time ago."

"Last stranger?" asked Sarah.

"Yes," said Tazmaz. "Many cycles ago, a stranger from your land came here. She stayed with us for thirty-six cycles. When she left, the trouble started soon after. We woke one morning to find our lands full of the Takers. They did not bother us till there was no life left in our land."

"What stranger? Who?" asked Sarah.

"A young female like you. Her name was Stephanie. She was found out in the blue forest, but she had to stay here with us till the passage in the maze opened so we could send her back to where she should be."

"Stephanie," said Sarah, "I have an Auntie Stephanie. She used to live here. Well, not here, but in Grandma's. Anytime we asked her about the bramble maze, she would change the subject and tell us never to go there. But she would not take anything." *Could it be the same Stephanie?* Sarah thought to herself.

"And she stayed here in this cave with you?" asked Sarah.

"No," said Tazmaz, "we lived on the land. Our land was pure back then, and we had no troubles. We all lived in the open. We had a village where the young played without any fear, and the females could go and collect fruit anytime they wanted, not when they were told. This was the thirteenth cycle of the fourth sun. This was when the stranger came to our lands and when the trouble started. Stephanie stayed with us for thirty-six cycles. When she had left back through the maze, not even a full cycle had passed, and then the Takers came."

"So if the Takers came because a thorn was lost, what happened to the thorn? I mean, where is it?" asked Sarah.

"We don't know. Only the wise man can answer that," said Tazmaz.

"Wise man? What wise man?" asked Sarah.

"There is a wise man that lives in the heart of the swamp. He is the only one who can tell us what to do and the only one that knows where the thorn is and how it must be replaced back to where it belongs. But for now, we must all rest."

Slowly they all left the fire and went to their sleeping areas.

Sarah looked around. She started to gather some straw to make a pillow and some sort of bed for herself. One of the females brought over some more straw and dropped it beside Sarah.

"Here, this will help you be a little more comfortable."

"Thank you," said Sarah. But the female said nothing and returned to her sleeping area.

Sarah lay down and looked at the fire. She thought to herself, *This is a right mess I have gotten into. Grandma will kill me.*

She could not rest easy. Her hair was up in a bun, and it was uncomfortable, so she sat up and undid her hair. With nowhere to put her hairpin and clips, she put them into her bag, and dozed off asleep, thinking of the trouble she was in and how was she going to explain all this to Steven and Louis and more so to Grandma where she was and how she got here. *Nobody was ever going to believe this story, so what's the point? I mean, Earth Keepers and Takers and black grass, trees, and fields and missing thorns. What next? Oh well, that's tomorrow.* She thought of the day's events that she had gone through and trying to get into her head how this all happened and how she ended up here.

She started off this morning looking for adventure with Steven and Louis. She had lived for today, the first day of her holidays. Today was supposed to be the first day of the big adventure they had planned this for months.

But instead, here she is, in a strange place with all sorts of funny-looking creatures, everything black or gray, water that smells, things that take your life, things that plant, swamps, and wise men. *Oh, I give up, this is all a dream, and soon I will wake up and be back with Steven and Louis in the maze.* But never in her wildest dreams did she ever think of what lay in store for her.

She started to doze off. Her eyes getting heavy, her mind racing back over things that had happened during the day, and so much had happened, and they happened so quickly—how she ended up here and how much trouble she was in—and then slowly she fell asleep.

Steven and Louis

"Did we look down this way, Steven?"

"I think we did, I am not sure. And everything looks the same in here."

"Look," said Steven, "why don't we mark each way that we go so we don't keep going in circles, which I think we have done, gone in circles that is, 'cause this looks like where we started half an hour ago."

"Yes, that's okay with me," said Louis. "But mark it with what?"

"I don't know."

"Okay, have you anything in your pockets?" asked Louis.

"No. Well, some change, matches, a penknife, that's it."

"The penknife we can mark the bushes as we go. You know, nick them so we will know the marks that we put on the bushes."

"Okay, suppose it's worth a try."

"Right," said Louis, "we will mark the bushes at each turn, then we will know which way we went so we don't have to check it again."

"Okay," said Steven, "we will start from there and mark as we go."

"Okay, well, we know we came this way, so mark it with an arrow pointing down to the ground."

"Why don't we start from here? You know, in case we missed a turn back there?"

"Okay," said Louis, "why not?"

"Okay, let's get started."

Louis and Steven started off again; this time marking the bushes as they went.

"You know what, Steven?"

"What, Louis?"

"Don't ask me to speak to her when we find her. She can spend the rest of the holiday playing with her dolls and things. I am never going with her to the brambles again."

"Let's just find her first and find out what happened to her and where she is. Then we can all relax and enjoy our holidays together. I mean, that's what we came here for. To have fun and get away from Mom and Dad, to be able to do our own thing for the holidays, not to spend the day looking for Sarah."

"Girls, I can't be bothered," said Louis.

"Yes," said Steven, "you're always getting into trouble over girls."

"Yes, I am, even that time in school when Joan got into trouble, and she decided to block all the toilets in the girls' section and stood there flushing them one after the other. There was water everywhere, all because the teacher told her she was sending a letter to her parents over her behavior in the school."

"Mary Callaghan came running out to the school yard and over to us to tell us what was happening. Like a fool, I ran back into the school and down to the toilets. All the girls were standing outside the girls' toilets. When I went into the girls' toilets, there was water everywhere. I started to drag Joan out, I never saw Mr. Downey behind me. All I heard was, 'What do you think you're doing, Louis?' Before I could say a thing, Joan said, 'Mr. Downey, I was trying to stop him, he has water everywhere,' and she started to cry.

"And Downey says to Joan, 'It's okay, Joan, you go back to the yard with your friends, and you'—he was pointing at me—'to the headmaster's office. You're going to pay for this one, Louis. I have been waiting for this day.'

Even Mom and Dad did not believe me when I told them what happened. I was grounded for two months. I mean, two whole months, no TV, nothing, school to bed to school."

"Yes," said Steven, "but when Joan was caught doing it again three weeks later, they all believed you then."

"Oh, that was grand. I had been grounded for them three weeks before she was caught. It does not matter who believed me then, I was the one who had paid for something I did not do for three weeks and all that jeering I got in school every day. That's what I am saying. Girls, all they do is cause trouble. Who needs them?"

"Well, whatever, so can we start looking for Sarah now?"

Louis looked toward the sky. "I suppose."

"Good," said Steven. "But you did not pay for anything. Don't forget, when Dad found out you were blamed in the wrong, he felt so guilty he went off and got you, what was it you got, Louis? Oh yes, a brand-new Xbox for your bedroom and your own TV and three games. I had to wait for my birthday to get one and Christmas for the TV. And you would not even let me play on yours for weeks."

"You only wanted to play it when you saw me on it. Every time I asked you if you wanted to play, you were too busy, so don't blame me. Can we go looking for Sarah now?"

Steven said nothing. What was the point? He was never going to win with Louis. He had an answer for everything, and according to him, he was always right. There were no middle areas, just everything was according to Louis and, if you did not like it, tough.

The Fifth Thorn

Sarah woke, things were blurred, and she was stiff and sore. She opened her bag and took out her clips and brush. When she started to focus, Tazmaz was standing in front of her, and to his right was Taz, and all around them was all the rest of the clan or most of them. They were all staring at her.

Sarah sat up rubbing her eyes. "Is something wrong?"

Tazmaz pointed at Sarah's hand. "Where did you get that?"

"Get what?" Sarah asked in amazement.

"That in your hand."

Sarah looked at her hand.

"This?" she said, holding up the hairpin and some clips and a brush. "You can't be talking about these."

"Yes," said Tazmaz, "I am."

"It's a hairpin and hair clips and a brush."

"No, it's not the clips. It's the hair pin. It's the missing thorn, it's the thorn that went missing a long time ago."

"No," said Sarah, "it's a hairpin. I have this years as far back as I can remember."

"Can you remember where you got it?" asked Tazmaz.

"No, I always had it, like, forever. You must be mistaken, and it's a hairpin, like a hair clip. You know, for your hair, to hold your hair in place like this."

Tazmaz sat down in front of Sarah. "I know what it might look like to you, but this is the missing thorn. But this is not the problem that we have. We somehow have to get the thorn back to its rightful place, and this can only be done by bringing the thorn to the wise man in the swamp."

"We?" asked Sarah. "We? Does that mean me?"

"Yes," said Tazmaz, "because an outsider took the thorn from its place, only an outsider can put it back. We will do all we can to get you there, but you must replace the thorn."

"I will go with her," said Taz.

"As will I," said Kak, who looked like Taz's twin brother.

About thirty-five more Earth Keepers said they would go; they almost all looked the same as one another.

"Quiet now," said Tazmaz. "I will pick four of you to go with Sarah, and you will all leave after food. You must travel fast and light, and you will have to get your own food as you go. Now eat."

"Hang on, I never said I was going. The only going I want to do is go home, not to some other part of Mogieland to put a hairpin anywhere. Well, except back into my hair."

"Sarah, you have to try to understand that if this thorn is not replaced, then all you see here will be gone, even us."

Sarah looked around the cave. All the Earth Keepers were standing, looking at her, She felt guilty. "Okay, I will do it."

Sarah did not feel so hungry now, but Taz told her she would have to eat now as they did not know when they would eat again.

Sarah forced herself to eat, but once she started to eat, she found she could not stop. The fruit was like nothing she had ever tasted before.

"Hymn, that is good," she said to Taz.

Sko just looked at Sarah then looked up to the roof.

"My, she can put away a lot," he muttered. "If she eats any more, we will have to carry her all the way to the wise man."

Tazmaz just looked at Sko. He did not have to say anything.

Sko stopped talking and started eating. Tazmaz looked at Sarah.

"Before you go, you have to know that the journey to the swamp is dangerous. You will see things you have never seen before, so you must follow all instructions from Taz, and you must follow them to the letter.

"When you get to the swamp, you will find the wise man, who will tell you where the thorn goes, but that's all the help you will get from the wise man. Speak to the caretaker, he can help you put the thorn back. He is the only one that can help you to replace the thorn, and the only one who can come and go at will in the wise man's lands. He is not bound by rules. The gatekeeper can get you to and from a point, but he cannot help you in any way, except advice."

"What caretaker? What gatekeeper?" asked Sarah.

"You will see them when and if you get to the wise man's lands to the north in the swamp."

Sarah just looked at Tazmaz. "What do you mean when and if?"

"Try not to worry. It seems a lot to understand, but the Earth Keepers will do all they can for you, and they will protect you with their lives if need be, but they can only go as far as the wise man. With their lives, this just gets better and better."

"Yes, and I wish you luck on your journey, and remember to follow all the instructions from Taz. It's for your own good."

"Thank you, Tazmaz," said Sarah. "I promise I will."

"Well, we best get started," said Taz.

Sarah and the four Earth Keepers got ready to start their journey.

Sarah looked around the cave and at all the faces of the Earth Keepers. She started to feel sorry for them and all that has happened to them because of the hairpin or thorn. If it is the missing thorn, then all this was caused by her family. Then she wondered, was this all suppose to happen? Was this some sort of plan? Was this a test for her? Was she going to ever get out of here? Was she ever going to get out of here alive, or was she going to be trapped here forever?

"Well, if Stephanie was here, and she went home, well then, I will get home as well. But I can't believe that Stephanie took the thorn, there must be a mistake somewhere."

"Stephanie would give you her last penny, and she would only do you a turn if it was a good one."

"No way, there has to be more to this than I am being told. There's no way Stephanie took anything from anywhere, it's totally not like her."

"But something has gone wrong here in Mogieland to cause all these problems, and someone would answer for all this."

But she was sure in her heart that Stephanie had nothing to do with it.

Sitting around the fire, looking at all these faces, she knew she had to try and restore some of what used to be for their sakes. Otherwise, they would be doomed to live forever in caves under the rule of the Takers. And if it's within her power, she would not let this happen. They deserve a better life than that; they need to return to the way they were before all this happened. Sarah had no idea what happened here in Mogieland or how she was going to help or what she was going to do. But with darkness all the time, like the way it is before a storm, well, that's not right. These Earth Keepers need to be back out in the open; they need to get their lives back and their freedom. After all, it's only right. And the land needs to be restored back to normal with proper color. It needs to be fresh and green. If the Earth Keepers' lands were anything like Annie's gardens, you could get the smell of the flowers as soon as you entered the gate into the garden and the colors of all the different flowers or like the smell of Grandad's apple trees. No wonder they were all so sad they needed to get back out on the land.

The Takers

The place was cold, there was no fire, and they all sat everywhere. They all looked alike; they did not look a bit like the Earth Keepers. They were black with evil red eyes and bony-shaped heads and skinny bodies, like they had been starved.

"Something is wrong," said Malgit. Malgit was the leader of the Takers. He was the biggest evil-looking thing ever seen. He stood about twelve feet, while the rest were only three to four feet high. Malgit had dark red eyes, like bloodred, and a short temper, which made him very dangerous, even to his own people.

"Something is wrong." He could feel it right down to his bones, and he could smell the change in the air.

"Go check the workers, count them. Bring Tazmaz here to me. I want to know what they're up to. Send some of my army to the swamp, check that the wise man and the caretaker if they are still there and what they're up to. Go, go now. On second thought, no, wait. I will go to Tazmaz myself. I need nourishment, and if I don't get the answers I want, he may just be the source of nourishment that I need. Some of you go to the wise man's lands. Check and see if things are as they should be."

There was a scurry. Takers ran in all directions to get out of the way of Malgit, for it was not unknown to him to turn on his own and suck their life force from them just for the sake of it. He ruled the Takers with pure fear.

Malgit stood up. His size and height were impressive. He let out a roar, which shook the very ground on which he stood.

"Go!" he roared at the Takers. "Don't stand around looking at each other. Do as I told you. Go, go now!"

As he started to move, something caught his eye. A small furry thing about the size of a rabbit ran past him. As fast as it was—and it was fast—Malgit was even faster.

It was in his hand before a blink of an eye.

Malgit held it in front of him and looked at the little furry animal. As he did, Malgit's eyes started to glow a bright bloodred. His grip tightened around the little animal. The little animal's color started to fade first to light gray then gray. In seconds, it was black. Malgit tossed the animal aside. It was dead. The life drained from it.

"That was good, it will keep me going for a short while." Malgit started off in the direction of Tazmaz's camp. There was a lot he wanted to know, and he would find out one way or another. Malgit instructed forty of his Takers to go ahead of him to Tazmaz's and watch.

"You are to do nothing. If there was anything odd happening there or anything out of place, I want to know as soon as I arrive at Tazmaz's. Fail me on this," he said as he studied the faces of the ones he picked, "and you will pay for your failure with your lives. Now go!"

Malgit looked around. He had thousands of Takers in his army.

He had spent a lot of time and effort getting to where he is, and he was going to hold on to the power he gained no matter what the cost.

Life here as a leader was good, too good to lose his leadership. He had to answer to nobody, and his word was law and final, and any Taker who disobeyed him paid a dear penalty, which was final. It was death. There was no lesser penalty accepted under his rule, none. If he showed any sign of weakness, it would be his own downfall, and there were plenty of young

Takers ready to take his place. But only fear kept them at bay, and that's the way he was going to keep it.

"Right, you all know what you have to do. Check all the lands from here to the north of our lands and to the south of the Earth Keepers' land. And anything that does not look or sound right, I want to know. No matter how small it might seem to you, I want to know. Now go cover all the lands in Mogieland, and that means everywhere. From the top of our lands to the bottom of the Earth Keepers' lands, even the lands of the Clickers and the Vox."

One young Taker asked, "Malgit, is it not too dangerous to go to the land of the Clickers? If we go to the land of the Clickers, we will be killed."

Malgit reached out and caught the young Taker by the throat. Malgit looked into his eyes and squeezed. The young Taker turned black. "This is what happens to anybody who questions me." Malgit dropped the young Taker to the ground.

"And if you don't, you will die by my hand anyway. Now that I have made myself quite clear, go!"

The Takers left to search the lands. They were not happy, and there was a lot of talk among them as they left. But not one of them wanted to or had the power to challenge Malgit, so they had no choice but to follow his instructions.

The Vox

Sarah sat looking at these four funny-looking, funny-faced molelike animals. She thought to herself, *If this Malgit is as bad as they say he is, how are they going to help me?*

As Sarah started to get up, a sound like thunder, maybe a roar, but whatever it was, shook the ground.

"Time to go," said Taz. "Malgit knows you're here. There's no time to lose. We have to get you to the blue forest, you will be a little safer there as Malgit is still wary of the Vox."

"The who?" asked Sarah.

"The Vox."

"What are the Vox?" asked Sarah.

"They are the creatures that live in the blue forest. Malgit, for some reason, won't cross them. He will only go into the blue forest if he has to. Otherwise, he sends in the Takers to do what he wants. He is the same when it comes to the land of the Clickers."

"Clickers, what are they?"

"I have no time to tell you everything. I want you to be careful. You have to go now. These four Earth Keepers will go with you to the wise man's lands in the swamp to see the wise man. They will keep you safe till you get there. Sarah, you know Taz. This is Miz, Sko, Wapz. These are the Earth Keepers that will travel with you."

"How do I tell them apart?" asked Sarah.

"Oh, you will," said Tazmaz. "Now go."

Sarah put her hair back up in a bun and put the pin back into her hair.

"Okay, I suppose I'm as ready as I will be. Let's go."

They left the cave, keeping a watchful lookout for Takers and started on the first leg of their journey.

The Earth Keepers watched till they disappeared out of sight. Then they returned to whatever it was they were doing before Sarah and the four Earth Keepers left.

"It's up to them now," said Tazmaz, shaking his head. "Our faith is in their hands. Okay, everybody, return to work and not a word of any of this to anybody, not even your friends in the other clans."

Tazmaz looked back across the fields again.

"And please be swift."

But he had a feeling that this was only the start of a lot of trouble.

The Blue Forest

All five left the cave and headed across the fields toward the blue forest. Looking back, they could see Tazmaz and the Earth Keepers waving to them. They did not wave in case anybody was watching. Keeping close to the hedge rows, they could see the Earth Keepers working in the fields in the distance, and they could also see the Takers who were watching the Earth Keepers working.

Just before the start of the forest, they came to a stream. Sarah stopped. Seeing the crystal clear water made her feel thirsty.

"I need a drink," said Sarah.

"Okay," said Miz, "but make it quick."

"Okay." Sarah bent down to get a drink. She noticed the water. It looked funny. It was so clear she never saw water like it before. She took a drink.

"Oh, that tastes so good."

Miz said, "It's the pure water of all the lands. That's why the grass, trees, and everything grows so fast. The water comes from the mountains, from an underground cave. It runs through a crystal cave, and it carries some of the power of the crystals."

"Well, it tastes good," said Sarah. "And I don't care where it comes from. All I know is I am thirsty, and this is the best water I have ever tasted."

"Well, I am glad you like it. But we have to go," said Miz.

And they started into the blue forest. The growth in the forest was very thick. But Sko, who was leading, seemed to be following a path. But it did not stop the bushes slinging back at Sarah and slapping her in the face and head.

"Be careful," she called out. Sarah noticed that the stream ran back into the blue forest and vanished underground.

The Earth Keepers were smaller than her, so they were able to stay under the big branches and move faster than her.

"Hay, slow down a little," said Sarah.

Wapz slowed.

"Sarah, you have to keep up. It's very important that we get to the center of the forest before the Takers know we are here," said Taz.

"Why is it so important?" asked Sarah.

"Because they will do anything to stop us once they know what we are doing, so we will have to try and keep ahead of them. Now come on and try to go a little faster," said Taz.

They were making good time when they came to a small clearing. They stopped at the edge.

"Wait," said Sko.

"What now?" said Sarah.

"Wait and be quite, please."

"Oh, whatever. Hurry, hurry, then wait. Make up your minds."

There were two boulders right in the middle of the clearing.

Wapz let out a small sound, like when someone gargles.

Sarah's eyes widened. No, this can't be real. The boulders started to move apart, leaving a gap between them.

"Now," said Miz, "run."

"No, wait," said Taz.

They all stopped and looked at Taz.

"Oh, here we go again," said Sarah.

Taz pointed across the clearing. Beyond the boulders, there were five—no, there were six—Takers on their way across the bottom field.

The Takers were dragging two of the Earth Keepers with them. The Earth Keepers were trying to struggle and crying out for help.

Sarah could hear their cries from where she was. It was sickening to listen to.

"Come on," said Sarah.

"Come on what?" said Taz.

"Come on, let's go and help them."

Taz looked at Sarah with sad eyes.

"I am sorry, but there's nothing we can do for them. Once the Takers have one of us, there is no one that can help us, and if we go to help, they will kill us. And you will be captured and that will be the end of everything."

Sarah just bit her lip.

"And you're supposed to be protecting me. How can you protect me when you can't do anything for your own kind? I hope I don't have to depend on you the way your friends do. Now that would make me feel really safe."

Taz looked at Sarah.

"Your safety is what matters, nothing else. Even if it means letting all our friends die, then so be it. If I could help our friends and keep you safe at the same time, then I would. But I can't, and I won't risk your safety for nobody."

Sarah just looked at Taz. She said nothing.

They waited for a few minutes till the Takers vanished with the two screaming Earth Keepers, and it was safe for them to go on.

The Crystal Cave

The Takers vanished across the field as soon as the way was clear.

They all ran toward the boulders.

Miz headed for the center of the boulders.

As they got closer, there was a small opening on the ground.

All four Earth Keepers and Sarah ran into the opening and down into a tunnel. It was very bright in the tunnel.

The boulders moved back across the opening.

Miz stopped then Taz and Wapz, and Sarah ran into Sko.

"Oops, sorry," said Sarah.

"It's okay," said Sko.

The opening was now closed.

"How come it's not dark in here?" asked Sarah.

"Crystals in the walls, they give off the light."

"The same as the diamonds in your cave."

"They're not diamonds, they're crystals," said Taz.

"Look, they're everywhere," said Sarah to Wapz.

"Yes, I know."

"It looks like stars, only brighter."

"Yes, they are the underground light and heat."

As they walked farther into the cave, they came to an open area.

"Ah, nice," said Sarah. "Where do we go now?"

"Nowhere," said Taz. "Now we rest."

Sarah sat with her back against the wall, facing the way they had come in. The wall behind her was warm. As she sat there, she noticed something odd—well, funny. There were two little animals about eight-ninth inches tall, like worms, only fatter and pinker.

They seemed to be talking to each other. Sarah got up and went over to them to get a closer look. When she got near, the two animals turned toward Sarah and started to turn purplish. They also started to grow and spin. Sarah stepped back. She could feel the heat from them.

It started to go from warm to warmer.

Sarah stepped back a little farther, but it was still getting warmer, and the animals were growing to double their size.

Sko ran over between Sarah and the two animals. He muttered something that Sarah did not understand. The two animals started to shrink, and their color went back to pinkish.

Sko looked at Sarah. "You're very lucky, they are the Vox. If they got to full height, they would have burned you to ashes. That's why the Takers leave them alone. If one of them is hurt, they come in their thousands to avenge the one who was hurt. Now please go and rest. We have a very busy day tomorrow with little or no time to rest. We have a lot of land to travel. And we need to be ready."

Sarah felt very alone for the first time in her life.

Sarah wondered where Steve and Louis were and what they were doing now. Were they looking for her? Had they told Annie she was missing? Did they even notice she was gone? Well, they would have noticed by now. Was her mom and dad in Nana's looking for her? Had they cancelled their flight to Spain?

And was Grandma home? Were they looking for her?

Had grandma told Sarah's mother that she was missing? Well, she must have done by now. It's been over twenty-four hours now. She remembered a time when a hiker went missing in the downs. The guards and all the locals spent two days and nights looking for him. And at the end of all that time, he was in a bed and breakfast. Oh god, were they all out looking for her?

"If Mom had to cancel her trip to Spain, I may as well stay here in this land forever because my life would not be worth nothing if I went home."

Were they all out searching for her?

Boy was she in trouble.

Sarah guessed she was in Mogieland a full twenty-four hours.

"They will all kill me when I get home, if I get home. I will be grounded, forever. If Steven and Louis had stayed with me, they would be here now, with me. Or maybe I would not be here at all. I would be in the brambles having an adventure with the two lads or most likely be at home, snug in my bed now. Not lying on the ground in a cave with things that can burn you to death in seconds or evil-looking creatures all around the place, waiting to suck the life out of everything that's living. And it seems that I am on the top of their menu."

Sarah was now feeling scared and alone. This was the first time that she has ever been away from home, except for Nana's. She felt totally alone; she could not even go to the shops on her own unless Mom or Dad went with her.

She just wanted to go home; she wanted to be back with the lads in the brambles having their battles or snug in her bed with her belly full of Nana's apple pie.

Sarah put her head back against the wall; it was warm. She started to cry to herself, not for any reason other than the fact that she was lonely and scared. She cried till she fell asleep.

The four Earth Keepers sat across from Sarah watching her, wondering what she was doing, why was she talking to herself, and why was she crying.

They knew this was all strange to her, and she felt out of place.

Then they watched as tears rolled down her face.

And then they watched as she slowly fell asleep.

And they knew that she must be sad and missing her own kind, but till the thorn is replaced, there was nothing they could do for her except try to keep her safe and alive as there was a lot of new surprises in store for her. And they hoped that she would be ready for them.

The four of them watched and said nothing till Sarah fell asleep.

Then they made themselves as comfortable as possible, and they went to sleep. Tomorrow would be a long and hard day for them all, and plenty of rest is what they all needed now.

The Crystal Translator

When morning came, Sarah woke. She felt warm and comfortable. It took her a few seconds before she remembered where she was. Sarah sat up and looked around the cave. It was still the same as before she went to sleep the night before.

Sko came over to Sarah.

"This is for you," said Sko.

"What is it?" asked Sarah, looking at this stone thing on a rope.

It looked like a small crystal, but without the shine.

"It's to protect you. It will also help you to understand the creatures when they talk," said Sko.

"Okay, thanks. Now I have two of these, this one and the one Taz gave me." She put it into her bag.

"You're welcome," said Sko. "Now, if you're ready, we have to meet with the leader of the Vox."

"Why?" asked Sarah.

"To get safe passage through the blue forest," said Sko.

They went to join the other three Earth Keepers.

All five stood together. From down a passageway, they could hear a crunching noise. It slowly got closer and closer till it was almost upon them. From out of the passage came a Vox, not like the ones Sarah had seen last night. But this one was about ten feet long, but it was dark purple. It had no arms or legs. It slid along like a giant worm. He had six—no, eight; no, ten—eyes. No, it's six. Sarah gave up. Every time she had them counted, more would appear, and some would disappear.

There was no point in trying to count them. Sarah stood with the four Earth Keepers. The Vox stopped in front of her.

There was a funny smell from the Vox; it smelled like rotten food.

Sarah's stomach started to turn; she felt like she was going to get sick.

"Why have you come here?" asked the Vox, addressing Taz.

Sarah took the crystal from her bag and put the crystal around her neck.

Taz replied, "We have come to see the wise man and the caretaker in the swamp, and we need your help."

Sarah could now understand what was been said.

"Why do you need to see the wise man?" asked the Vox.

"We need to find out how to replace the missing thorn."

"Oh, I see. How I can help?" asked the Vox.

"First, this is from Tazmaz." Taz put the drum of salt on the ground in front of the Vox.

"Thank you, now what can I do for you?"

"We need a crystal of light and any other crystals that you can give us to help us and safe passage through your lands."

The Vox seemed to freeze; he did not breathe or move.

After a few minutes, the Vox started to reach, as if it was getting sick.

Woop, woop. Then a load of goo came out of his mouth. It was like yellow spit, and in the middle of it, something was shining. Taz reached forward and picked up the shining object.

"Thank you," said Taz.

Sarah nearly vomited.

The Vox bent forward and tuck up the drum of salt in his mouth.

The Vox just turned and started back down the passageway. Taz walked over to a bowl of water and washed the object and put it in a pouch around his neck.

Taz came back over to where Sarah and the Earth Keepers were standing. "Okay, we have what we came for."

"Right, we can go now. We have what we need."

"What's with the salt?" asked Sarah.

"The Vox dig for salt to keep them alive, but there's not a lot of salt in the ground. And their bodies need salt."

"Okay," said Sarah.

They all headed to the place where we came in and waited.

Sko made a low sound, and the opening started to open.

"It's time," said Taz, "to start the next part of our journey. We have to get to the swamp to see the wise man, and maybe he can help us to replace the fifth thorn in its rightful place."

Yes, Sarah thought to herself, *maybe then this bad dream will end. No, not a dream, a nightmare. The quicker we get this done, the quicker I can get back to Grans and have some peace and put all this behind me. This place is really odd, and I don't like it one bit. If I had known this was in store for me, I would have stayed at home with Mom and Dad and went to Spain.*

Well, maybe not, but I would have not rambled off from Steven and Louis. Ah well, what's done is done. Maybe the faster we get this thorn back in its place, the sooner I will get home, and then I can start my real holidays, if there's any holidays left by the time I get out of here. And if I am allowed to go to Nana's ever again, maybe it would be safer to stay here.

Angela

Angela sat on the garden swing.

"Hello, my little angels," she said to a group of rosebushes. "You all look very well today." She turned and looked at the blossom tree to her right. "And my, do you look fine as well, my dear." Looking around the garden, she was happy with all her plants and trees. They were coming on very well.

She had spent a lot of time on her garden and put in a lot of hard work. But like everything, hard work pays. She remembered when she moved here first. The gardens were a field of brambles and weeds. It had taken a long time to clear the gardens and get them to where they were now. Ah yes, it was worth every blister and sore back.

Yes, she said to herself, *this is my garden.*

Local folk wondered how she could make things grow so fast and perfect. Some of them said it was a gift, others said she was a witch, and some said they had heard she sits in the forest at night talking to strange creatures. Some of them asked her for help with their gardens, but Angela just ignored them all. She was far too busy to listen to gossip or help people who would talk about her later.

"Well, my babies, I have something to do. I won't be long. But this cannot wait, and there is no time to lose. I will see you all later."

Angela went to the garden shed at the bottom of the garden.

"Now I am sure I left it in here. Well, I will soon find out."

Angela entered the shed and started looking at the shelves.

"Grandad has everything in here. It's going to be hard to find what I am looking for with all Grandad's stuff all over the place. Now where did I put it? It's been so long since I needed it. I know it's here somewhere." She lifted a cardboard box. "No."

She moved the garden hose. "No."

It's always in the last place you look. Looking behind Grandad's toolbox. "Ah, there it is." Picking it up, she dusted it. "Ah, still as good as new." She kissed it.

"Long time no see, I never thought I would have see you again," said Angela. Angela got a small cloth from the top shelf, cleaning it and wrapping it carefully and holding it close to her chest.

"Now, my little darling, we have things to do, and time is short."

Angela left the shed, locking the door and placing the key over the door. *That's silly,* she thought to herself, *locking a door and putting the key where everyone could find it. What's the point in locking the door in the first place? Grandad and his rules.*

She started across the garden stopping to pull up some weeds from around the heather.

"Now, pet, that will make you feel better," she said to the heather. "You will be able to breathe now."

Angela went out the garden gate and across the field. When she got to the river, she started walking upstream, humming away to herself. She carried on for about a mile till she came to some stepping-stones where she crossed over the river, which was a stream now, and to the edge of the forest. She walked along the forest edge, along a path, which was almost covered with weeds and moss. She walked for a short while till she came to a clearing. Angela entered the clearing. Over to the left was a pile of stones. Angela walked over to the stones, taking the first layer of stones of the top of the pile. She placed her hand inside the stones. Taking her hand out and looking at the crystal in her hand, she said out loud, "Now, my little darlings, we are ready." Returning to the center of the clearing, she knelt down, unwrapping it from the cloth and placing it on the ground.

She placed the crystal from the stones on top and waited.

The two items were crystals of different colors. Both crystals were now glowing.

When the two were put together, they started to glow even stronger.

As Angela watched, the glow got bigger and wider.

The grow started to engulf Angela.

It felt so good, she could feel all her aches and pains start to go. Looking at her hand, which she had cut two days before, the sore started to glow, then it vanished. Annie could see everywhere. She had to turn the top crystal in the direction that she wanted to go and just take the crystal away when she got there. She did not know what lay ahead, but she felt it was not good.

It was warm and comfortable. She felt like she had ten years taken off her age. She felt a lot younger and ready for what lay ahead.

It's been a long time since she used the crystals.

Angela felt herself being pulled into the glow.

She sat and relaxed and let herself go.

Angela felt everything start to spin.

All of a sudden, Angela felt a hand on her shoulder.

Angela turned. It was Louis.

"Annie."

Louis and Sarah

Steven and Louis were sitting on the ground, looking at each other. They had decided that if they stay very quiet, they might hear Sarah calling out or hear her going through the brambles.

Louis thought it was a stupid idea, but he was willing to give anything a go at this stage. After all, they had spent the last hour and a half looking for her and could not find her. He just wished they could find Sarah. He missed her, but he would never tell her that, ever.

He remembered the day he went to her house, and they were playing out the back. Sarah fell in the back garden and cut her knee. She ran into the house crying Grandad.

Grandad was at the cooker. The oven was on, and the door was open. Sarah's shoes were wet, and she slipped. She reached out to grab something to save herself. She caught the oven door. It was only for a few seconds, but it was plenty of time for Sarah to burn her hands. Before the pain hit, Grandad picked her up and put her hand under the cold tap for a long while.

But Sarah cried and cried, and Louis cried with her then, and for about two hours after, Grandad put a spray on Sarah's hands and gave her some Panadol after a few minutes, and she stopped crying.

But Louis and Grandad stayed with her all night. The next morning, Sarah had a big bubble on her hand. Louis cried for her because he could feel her pain, and her hand looked so sore.

A noise snapped Louis out of his thoughts. "What was that?" he asked.

"Oh, it was nothing," said Steven.

"Are you sure?" asked Louis.

"Yes," said Steven.

"Oh, okay."

Time

Steven was thinking to himself, *We will wait here for thirty minutes, then we will start searching again. After that, we will have to go home. And if Grandma is not home, we will have to tell Angela.* She might go mad, but he thought, what choice does he have now?

He wasn't going to worry; they still had plenty of time. You never know Sarah. She had a habit of turning up at the last minute.

"Did you bring anything to eat?" Steven asked Louis.

Louis started looking through his pockets and started to empty them out onto the ground in front of him.

Steven could not believe his eyes, three Mars bars, three Bounty bars, three packets of Skittles, three Twirls, and a bag of Jelly Babies,

"How did you get all that into your pockets?" asked Steven.

Louis shrugged his shoulders. "Don't know, just did. I have an idea," said Louis.

"Now what would that be?"

"Why don't I go back to the house and get Angela? She can help us look for Sarah. Three is better than two."

"Now for once, I have to admit, Louis, that's not a bad idea. Okay, so I will wait here, and you go and get Angela, and, Louis."

"What?"

"Don't get lost."

"Ha-ha, very funny," said Louis. "I won't be long, and I will even leave the chocolate here with you."

"Okay, thanks, Louis. I will be right here, and don't say too much to Angela. Just tell her that Sarah wandered off, and we can't find her in the maze."

"Well, that's what happened."

"Yes, but don't say anything else."

"Okay," said Louis. And he took off like the March Hare.

Louis ran for all he was worth through the brambles.

Bramble thorns were scraping him everywhere; he could feel the thorns pulling at his clothes as he ran through them.

Out into the forest, he was running so fast that he did not see a dip in the ground, and he ended up running in thin air for a few seconds before he came crashing down, cracking his butt on a tree stump. The pain ran right up to his head, and his bum stung like mad, bringing tears to his eyes.

"SARAH, I AM GOING TO KILL YOU WHEN I GET MY HANDS ON YOU!" he shouted.

He got up rubbing his butt, and the tears rolled down his face. After a second or two, he wiped the tears from his face and started running again, This time watching out for holes and hidden dips.

He was not going to crack his butt a second time today for nobody.

After ten minutes, he realized he had been going the wrong way.

Louis stopped, took a breath, and looked around, looking to the right and then to the left and back to the right.

"Ah, that's the way." Off he set again. After fifteen more minutes, he could see the edge of the forest. He could also see something strange. It's a light, and it's so bright and full of colors. He had never seen anything like it before. Confused, he headed for the light. When he could see the light, he could also see someone sitting in the light; but he could not make out who it was, that is, till he got close. *It's Angela. What's she doing? She looks like she's in a trance. I always knew she was a witch*, he thought to himself. He started to slow down till he was within arm's distance from Angela. He watched her for a few seconds. *This is really odd*, he thought to himself.

He put his hand out on Angela's shoulder. Bright colors flashed everywhere. He felt he was being dragged forward into something. He felt like he was spinning; then as fast as it all started, it stopped. The next thing he knew, he was at the edge of the forest with Angela. His hand was still on Angela's shoulder, but everything was different. Everything was black and white. Angela looked at Louis, and Louis looked at Angela.

Angela smiled. "Hello, Louis, welcome to Mogieland."

Louis just stood with his mouth open.

"And close your mouth, or you might get some unwelcomed guests in it."

"I will when you tell me just what happened, and where did you say we are? In what, monkey land?"

"Well, let's just say we went for a spin, and we are in a place called Mogieland."

"You're dead right there, Annie," said Louis and muttered. "I always knew you were a witch," he said under his breath.

"What was that, Louis?"

"I said you're dead, right?"

"Oh, I thought you said something else."

"Me? No, Annie, not me. That's all I said. Witch. Are you going to tell me how we got here, and why are we here? There has to be a reason why we are in this place."

"Yes, I will, but not now. It will have to wait till later. I have a lot to do, and seems you're here now, you can help me. And tell me, Louis, what you were doing in the north part of the forest when I thought you and Steven and Sarah were gone off to your camp?"

"Yep, Annie, I was on my way home to tell you that Sarah has gone missing. Steven lost her in the bramble maze."

"Ah now, two and two is making four."

"So why are we here, Annie?"

"Well, Louis, let's say that we are here for a reason, and you will understand more as we go along. And the other thing is, there's too much to tell you just now and no time to tell you."

"Yep, never time, whatever, but just tell me one thing."

"What?"

"Well, are there any shops here in monkey land because I am famished. I need to fill a spot."

"No, there are no shops here, but you will find plenty of fruits to eat."

"Ah, Annie, you have to be joking. I don't need fruit, I need a few bars of chocolate."

Annie just looked at Louis and smiled.

Louis muttered under his breath, "Witch."

"And name-calling won't help you either."

Louis turned red. *I can't believe she heard that, she has to be a witch.*

Annie turned to the right and started walking.

Louis followed. "It's always the same, adults don't care. I am going to die of hunger, and you get told, 'Here, have a banana, it's healthy.'"

The Takers and the Vox

The opening opened. Miz said to Sarah, "Keep close to me. When we leave here, it's not going to be safe for anyone."

"Okay."

But before they could move, Sko saw the Takers.

"Wait." All five stopped. "Look," said Sko, "over there." He pointed across to the next field to the right.

They all looked to where Sko was pointing.

"It's the Takers," said Taz.

"They are very far into the Vox lands," said Sko.

"It's not like them. There's something wrong when you see the Takers this far in the Vox's land," said Taz.

They watched and waited. There was nothing else they could do.

"They're heading this way," said Miz.

"Quiet, everybody," said Taz, "and keep down."

As the Takers were about four hundred meters from them, one of the Takers stopped and picked up something. He held it at arm's length, shaking it and turning it around.

The Taker's eyes started to glow.

The thing in the Taker's hand started to grow.

It grew fast and turned red, a bright red.

The Taker dropped the thing it was holding and started blowing on his hand, the way you do when you burn your hand.

The thing started to spin faster and faster.

The Takers started to back away, but they were far too slow.

The thing grew to three, maybe four, feet in seconds. It was spinning so fast, it was just a blur. Red jets of liquid spurted from it. Each jet directed at its target, a spray of the red liquid hit each of the Takers.

The Taker's skinny frames turned red, the liquid spread so fast over the Takers. After a few seconds, there was just a pile of ash.

All this took only a few seconds. From start to finish, the Takers had not even got time to call out.

The things returned to their normal size in seconds and burrowed back into the ground.

Sko turned to Sarah. "That's why the Takers are afraid of the Vox."

Sarah was left with her mouth open.

They left the cave and made their way to the forest's edge, watching all the time in case there were any more stray Takers around.

Once at the forest edge, Taz took out the crystal and held it up over his head.

He only held it over his head for a few seconds before a light came from the crystal, like a beam from a torch, and shone to a pathway into the forest. The pathway was covered with moss and weeds, but in the light of the crystal, you could see the stones under the moss.

"Okay," said Taz, "it's this way."

All five entered the forest, Taz was leading.

Taz put his hand on each tree as he passed.

Sarah thought she could hear the tree moan.

No, she said to herself, *I know it's just me.*

But she did notice that each tree they passed, the trees' branches leaned toward the Earth Keepers as if asking for help.

They travelled on down through the forest, passing all sorts of strange creatures.

They were making slow progress, but they dare not stop for the fear of coming across any Takers.

After a while, Sarah asked Miz, "Is it me, or is the ground getting softer? I am sinking into the ground."

Miz said, "No, it's not you. The ground is getting softer. We are nearing the swamp, it won't be long. We will be stopping for food soon."

They travelled about a mile when Sarah found it harder to walk. The ground was very soft now. Every step was a struggle, and she was sinking into it with every step. Her runners were covered in a blackish gray mud.

"Taz, slow down please," said Sarah. "I can't keep up with you. I am losing my runners, and if I lose my runners, well, that will be the end of this trip for me unless you want to carry me all the way to where it is we are going to."

"Okay," said Taz, "we will stop over there for food and a rest, but we can only stop for a short while."

"Okay, thanks," said Sarah. Sarah thought to herself, *Food? What food? We did not bring anything with us. We don't even have a bottle of water between us.*

Taz stopped and sat down. The other three Earth Keepers sat beside Taz.

"Sit here," said Taz to Sarah. "It's the driest place around."

Sarah sat beside Sko. There were lots of little animals running around. "What are they, Taz?"

Taz put his hand out, and one of the little animals ran over to him. Taz picked him up. "These little things are called Malic," he said as he raised it to his mouth.

"Taz, what are you doing?"

Taz put the animal back down. "Only joking," he snorted and laughed.

"Oh, I thought you were going to eat it. And what do you call them?" Sarah pointed at more little animals half the size of the Malic.

"Oh, them little things," said Taz, "they are Malic babies."

Now Sarah felt stupid.

The four Earth Keepers started to snort, wondering now where Taz was going to get food from here in the middle of nowhere with nothing around except wet ground and black everything else. *This should be good, and they need not expect me to eat anything that's living. Oh, to have a burger and chips now.* Now that sounded good or even a packet of crisps. That would even do for her, she would even settle for her dad's stew. And this time she would eat the stew with no hassle from her dad or smart comments from her. In fact, she was so hungry she would even eat Steven's scrambled eggs. And now that was saying a lot, and it was also very brave. But at this point, she was prepared to take the chance on Steven's eggs. She was terrified that these Earth Keepers were going to start eating crawly things from the ground, and she did not care how hungry she was. That would be where she would draw the line. She watched Taz to see what he was going to do and where he was going to get some food from. She thought to herself, *This should be good, and now my next trick is because he would want to do magic to get food here.*

Lunch

Taz took the crystal and placed it on the ground.

The crystal glowed for all twenty seconds. Taz picked up the crystal and put it back into his pouch.

Taz sat and watched the ground in front of him. After a few minutes, the ground started to shake.

Sarah jumped back a little. "What's happening?"

"It's okay," said Taz to Sarah. "There's nothing to be afraid of, just watch and see."

Sarah relaxed a little.

The ground started to open only a few inches, and fruit started to come up out of it. After a few seconds, when the food stopped coming out of the hole, a Vox stuck his head out. He just looked around, sniffed the air, and then went back down the hole.

"How did they do that?" asked Sarah.

"They have tunnels everywhere with storerooms placed along the tunnels. It's how they feed themselves with fruit and roots."

"No," said Sarah, "I mean, where do they get the fresh food from?"

"They have their own gardens underground where they grow things. In the light of the crystals, they are very good at growing things underground. Nearly as good as us, well, you could say they are as good as us underground.

They are able to feed themselves all the time. They also help us as you can see for yourself. And our food is very limited.

But they also eat little things as well."

"Like?"

"Like the little things that crawl around the caves. We call them Magwigs."

"Oh, I think I understand. More like maggots, that's what we call them."

"I think so."

"The crystals," asked Sarah, "what about them?"

"Oh yes, the crystals. They provide heat and light for the caves."

"Oh," said Sarah, "I think I understand how it works now. Thank you, Taz."

Taz washed the fruit and placed it on a dry leaf.

"Okay, now we all must eat."

They ate in silence, and when they were finished, Taz buried what was left.

"Are we ready to go?" asked Taz.

Then they started back on their journey.

"Why did you bury the food?" asked Sarah.

"Because the Takers can smell them, and before you would know it, there would be Takers all around. They can smell anything that has life."

"This far away?" said Sarah.

"Yes," said Taz, "this far away."

"Whatever," said Sarah.

Sarah was finding it a lot harder to walk as the ground was getting damper and damper, and her runners were soaking wet.

Twice she lost one of her runners and had to stop to dig it out of the mud. *If this ground gets any softer, I will end up with no runners at all.*

Looking at Taz's feet, she said to Taz, "I see you don't have that problem with shoes, do you?"

Taz looked down at his feet. "No, we don't." He made a gurgling sound.

I suppose that was a laugh as well as the sounds you made earlier, Sarah thought.

"It won't be much longer," said Taz, "till we get to the wise man's lands. There you will be able to rest and wash and have plenty to eat."

"Taz, tell me some more about this wise man and caretaker."

"There's not much I can tell you, Sarah. This is my first time to ever be near the wise man's lands. I have heard stories, but they were only stories."

"Okay, so what were the stories about?"

"Well, it's said that a long time ago, before even the land called Mogieland was one with only the Earth Keepers in the land. Something happened, and some of the Earth Keepers started to change. They no longer needed food, and their bodies got thinner, and they turned on the Earth Keepers. Then a wise man came into the lands from outside Mogieland. He divided the lands. He called the bad Earth Keepers Takers, and he banished them to the north. Then he put a forest across the bottom of their lands. After the forest, he placed a swamp with three safe paths across the swamp. Then he placed a second forest at the south of the swamp, and then you had the land that was left. That's our lands from the west to the east of the swamp.

"The wise man placed nine thorns. These thorns were made of special wood. Once all nine were placed in the ground, they created a special barrier, which could not be broken, and we all lived happy. That is until one of the thorns went missing. The fifth thorn and the barrier fell. Then the Takers had access to all the lands. The wise man put his home in the middle of the swamp, but you have to get permission to enter his land unless the gatekeeper brings you there. Other than that, there is no other way in to the wise man's lands.

"The three safe paths run close to the wise man's lands. These were paths made by the wise man for creatures to cross the swamp from one forest to the other, and if you did get into the wise man's lands, it is said that the wise man has creatures protecting his lands. And even the Takers and the Vox won't go up against it, for it is said that one of these creatures can kill one hundred Takers in seconds. Now, Sarah, this is what I have been told, and as I said, I don't know as I have never been there. But I think we are going to find out very soon."

"I hope they're on our side, Taz."

"So do I, Sarah, so do I. I would hate to think that we have come this far and not be allowed to enter the wise man's lands. If this was to happen, then I fear all would be lost."

"Is there no way we can contact the wise man to let him know that we are coming to see him?"

"The wise man knows everything, and I think and I hope that he already knows that we are coming to see him."

The Clickers

Sarah was third in line after Taz and Sko. She thought she heard something. She looked back just in time to see Wapz fly backward into the forest. She screamed at Taz. "Wapz, Wapz! He's gone, he went flying backward into the forest!"

Taz looked back just in time to see Wapz vanish into the forest.

Taz took out the crystal and held it over his head. A red light shone from it. Sarah felt heat from the light.

"We are safe now," said Taz.

"But what about Wapz?" asked Sarah.

"It's too late for Wapz," said Taz. "He has been taken."

"What do you mean taken?" said Sarah. "We have to get him back."

The three Earth Keepers looked at each other, shaking their heads. "It's too late," said Sko. "Nobody ever comes back from the Clickers."

"No!" screamed Sarah. "No, this can't be happening."

And she took off running in the direction where Wapz had disappeared to.

Sarah ran through the forest. She ran till her chest hurt. Her lungs screaming for air. Tears ran down her face as she called out over and over. "WAPZ, WAPZ, where are you? Answer me, Wapz."

She ran for what seemed like forever till she came to a clearing.

As she entered the clearing, she stopped dead. It took Sarah a few seconds to focus on what lay in front of her. When she realized what she was looking at, she backed up and hid behind a tree. It took her a few seconds to catch her breath, and then she peered around the tree to have another look and make sure she seen what she saw. When she realized what she was looking at was real, she felt so afraid. Sarah heard noises from behind her. She stooped down as low as she could and inched closer to the clump of bushes at the base of the tree. Sarah did not know what she was going to do now.

In front of her were flying scaly things with huge eyes and sharp long beaks and small claws. They had a tail with what looked like a ball halfway down and a long pin coming out of the end of the ball, like one of Grandma's knitting needles. They were nasty-looking things. No wonder the Takers were afraid of them.

They looked like giant bees but with scales and about two feet long.

They were everywhere.

The noise was now very close, like the sound of crickets.

The noise came close and *click click* and passed over her head. There were more of these flying things. There were about half the size of Sarah. Sarah watched as the ones that flew over her head headed for a mound in front of her.

She never noticed it before, but it was a small mountain, and they landed and went into the opening. Sarah watched for a while looking all around, taking in everything.

Sarah was trying to work how to get into the hive. She was sure that was where Wapz was. Sarah was so busy watching the flying things and that they were going into the opening but not coming out.

That was when something grabbed her shoulder. She nearly died of fright. Sarah looked around, terrified.

Taz was looking straight into her face.

"Don't ever do that again," said Sarah.

Taz put his finger over his lips. "Shush."

"What are you doing here?" asked Sarah.

"We have to stay with you and protect you. That's what Tazmaz instructed us to do. So whether we like it or not, we had to follow you. And we don't like it. This is not a safe place to be," said Taz.

Sarah looked at Taz. She could see the fear in his face.

"What are they?" She pointed at the flying things.

"They are the Clickers."

"They are the what?"

"The Clickers, they make a clicking sound when they fly, and they have a sting in their tails that can kill. They don't like anybody or anything. They attack everything and take you away to their hive. That is what we are told. Hardly anyone has ever come back after been caught by the Clickers.

"The Clickers were very protective of their areas, they let no one anywhere near. All the creatures in Mogieland stayed away from them and their area, for not to do so meant certain death. Even the Takers don't stand a chance when it comes to the Clickers. Nobody comes into the Clickers' lands, and if they do, they never leave. This is a bad place to be. Please, Sarah, come with us out of this place, so we can finish the job Tazmaz told us to do."

"You think I am leaving here without Wapz? Well, think again, Taz."

Sarah studied the area, watching to see if there was any way at all she could get into the hive. But from what she could see, there were Clickers going into the hive all the time. Then something odd happened. She noticed the Clickers were going into the hive, but they were not coming out. Maybe they were going into the hive for the night, or there was another place where they came out of the hive. She did not know, she would have to take things as they are because one way or another, she was not leaving here without Wapz no matter what the cost was. She watched and waited. This was something she had to do, and she expected no help from anyone else, and that included the Earth Keepers. She knew they were terrified, she could see it on their faces. She felt sorry for them,

The Rescue

"Well, Clicker or no Clicker, we have to get in there," said Sarah, pointing at the opening.

"No," said Taz, "we have to go, it's too dangerous here."

"No," said Sarah, "we have to get Wapz."

The Earth Keepers looked at each other, shaking their heads.

It was starting to get dark, and Sarah noticed that there were very few of the Clickers around, well, none. It seemed they had all gone into the hive for the night.

Sarah looked at the Earth Keepers. They we terrified. She looked at the opening, took a deep breath, and ran across the open area till she got to the opening, stopping for just a second to catch her breath. She snuck into the opening. She could hear a lot of noise, but it came from farther down. It was a single passage, which was twisty. Sarah followed the passageway, hoping she would not meet anything as she had nowhere to hide. As she went around the bend, she came to two openings. *What now?* she thought to herself. *Which way?* Sarah could hear noise coming from the left, but nothing from the right. She went right; she followed the opening for a few minutes when she came upon caves on both sides of the tunnel. They were cell-like rooms or more like cells.

She snuck from cell to cell, they were all empty. She came to the next turn. Just as she was about to go around the corner, she heard *click click*.

Sarah stopped dead. She looked around. There was nowhere to go. She squeezed herself tight to the tunnel wall, holding her breath.

Click, click, click. Two of the Clickers passed her.

Her knees started to shake.

One of the Clickers stopped very close to Sarah.

Sarah could hear her own breathing.

The Clicker started off down the tunnel again.

Sarah took a deep breath and started off again.

She turned left and came to the first cell. Sarah looked into the cell. She could see nothing. The place was so dark.

Moving on to the next and the next cell when she heard a sound, she stopped and went back to the fourth cell. Sarah looked into the cell again but could see nothing. It was pitch black in there.

Then she heard the low moan again over in the far corner. Still Sarah could see nothing. Sarah heard the sound again. She went into the cell. It was very dark in there, almost impossible to see anything.

Squinting her eyes, she could make out a shape over in the corner.

Sarah carefully moved over to where the sound was.

She could see Wapz. He was filthy, and Sarah ran over to him.

"Are you all right?"

"Yes," said wapz, "thank you."

Sarah helped him to stand.

As Wapz stood up, Sarah noticed he was hurt.

He was bleeding from his shoulder.

"You're hurt, you're bleeding," said Sarah.

"It's where the Clicker caught me."

"It looks sore."

"It's okay."

"Okay," said Sarah, "let's get out of here."

"Yes, please."

Wapz stood up and dusted himself down. "Ready."

"Okay," said Sarah, "let's go."

They both started on their way out of the hive.

They made their way back up along the tunnel, passing the cells around the bend till they came to where the tunnels joined.

"This way," said Sarah. Wapz followed Sarah.

Around more bends, they could see the light ahead.

"Nearly there now," said Sarah to Wapz.

Click, click, click. Sarah stopped.

There were two Clickers at the exit; they seemed to be guarding it.

"That's all we need now, guards."

They waited. Sarah was thinking, *What we are going to do?*

There was a noise at the entrance and a second loud bang. The two Clickers took off.

Sarah grabbed Wapz's hand and ran out of the hive across the open ground as fast as their legs could carry them and in behind the trees where the other three Earth Keepers waited.

The three of them grabbed Wapz and start hugging him.

"You're hurt," said Taz.

"It's okay," said Wapz.

Taz took the crystal from his pouch. He put the crystal over Wapz's wound. He moved the crystal in an up-and-down motion.

The crystal started to glow.

Taz held the crystal in place for a while.

When Taz took the crystal away, the wound was healed.

"Thank you," said Wapz.

Taz said nothing.

He rubbed Wapz's head.

"Okay, okay," said Sarah, "let's go. We have to get as far as possible away from here as quick as possible."

Sudden Death

The three Earth Keepers watched as Sarah ran across the open ground and into the entrance of the hive, The three of them stood frozen, for pure fear rooted them to the ground, for all three knew what was in the hive. Their fear was not because of the Clickers but the thing that controlled them. They had never seen what it was, but over the campfires, the stories that were told by the elders made their blood run cold. Once they were caught by the Clickers, that was it for the Earth Keepers. And the Takers that were caught, they never returned, except one Earth Keeper who escaped, but that was a long time ago, and the stories that he told were passed down from leader to leader for as long as anyone could remember,

They stood looking at each other, not knowing what to do.

They dare not go after Sarah, but if anything happened to her, they could not go back to their own camp and tell Tazmaz that they had failed. Everything depended on them: the return of normalcy in the lands, the thorn put back in its rightful place, and the return of the Takers to their own land.

None of them spoke, but they were all thinking the same thing.

They watched as the two Clickers took up guard positions at the entrance of the hive.

Miz shook Taz. "Look." He pointed at the entrance.

In the background, they could see Sarah; she was standing just inside the entrance with Wapz standing very close to her.

"She can't get out," said Sko.

Miz looked around. He picked up some stones and lobbed some of them off to the right of the Clickers.

The Clickers turned toward the sound of the noise.

Miz lobbed some more stones to the right.

The Clickers took flight, heading to the noise.

As soon as the Clickers took off, Sarah and Wapz came running out of the hive. They ran straight toward Sko, Miz, and Taz.

The three Earth Keepers were excited and terrified at the same time in case the Clickers came back, while Wapz and Sarah were running across the open ground.

Sko, Miz, and Taz armed themselves with more stones. Not that stones would be any good against the Clickers, but it might draw them away from Sarah and Wapz. It was a bad plan and a slim chance that it would work, but there was nothing else they could do except show themselves and hope the Clickers would go for them and leave Wapz and Sarah alone, and that's if the Clickers did not wake the whole swarm.

If they did, then they were in big trouble. None of them would get away if the swarm was woken, and that would be the end of replacing the thorn. With Sarah gone and the thorn gone and no chance of the thorn ever being replaced, Mogieland would be left in the control of the Takers, and that would be the end of any hope for his people. They would spend their days in total control of the Takers with never any hope of ever being free.

Marbles

Louis looked at Angela.

But before he could say anything, Angela said to Louis, "It's okay, honey, I will explain everything to you later. But not for now. We will have a lot of things to do and so little time to do them, so we have to do them fast. There is no time for me to explain all this to you just now. Now let me check where we are." Angela did a slow 360-degree turn.

Louis watched Angela, and he thought to himself, *If that's fast, I sure would hate to see slow.*

"Now, child, I know where we are."

"Good," said Louis, "that makes one of us."

Angela looked at Louis. "Well, child, we are in the blue forest."

"Don't you mean the black forest?"

"Something has gone wrong," said Angela. "This forest was so full of life the last time I was here. Now everything looks dead."

After a few seconds, Angela said, "The Takers, all this has to be because of them."

"The what?" said Louis.

"The Takers, I knew they would have had something to do with this. The life and the color is gone from everything. This place is destroyed. Everything is ruined, everything is gone."

"Yeah, and so is your marbles," muttered Louis.

"Right, let's go," said Angela, grabbing Louis by the hand. She headed for the swamp. She had heard what Louis had said this time.

"Where are we going?" asked Louis.

"Wait and see," said Angela.

"I don't like surprises," said Louis.

"Well then, this is not your lucky day because you won't like what's in store. There's a lot of don't-likes coming your way, so if I was you I would stay quiet and do as you're told. This is not a safe place to be, not for you and not for me. So the best thing you can do, Louis, is do as you're told and no more smart remarks. Do we understand each other? The sooner we sort out what is going on here, the sooner we can fix it, and I don't need any interference from you. This is going to be hard enough to sort."

"Yes, Annie." Louis knew he had overstepped the line, so for now, he was going to stay quiet. Well, for a while.

"Good, as long as we understand each other."

"Is there anything that I can do to help?"

"Yes, there is. You can work with me, and maybe—notice I am saying maybe—we can sort this out and restore things back to normal, but we need help. We need a lot of help."

"Help from whom?"

"Help from the wise man and the caretaker and from anybody else that we can get help from. This is not going to be an easy task."

Louis said nothing.

Steven

Steven had finished the third bar. He lay on his back looking at the sky, thinking out loud, "Louis should be at Nan's by now. I would hate to be in his shoes, having to tell Angela we lost Sarah. Angela will blow a fuse.

But then again, Louis is used to that. He is always getting into trouble."

Steven thought back to the day his dad painted Louis's bedroom. The paint wasn't even dry when Louis went into the bedroom and, with permanent marker, drew a full-sized Batman on the wall.

You could hear Dad calling Louis from about a mile away. Louis ran, but it did no good. Even now, Louis can't understand why Dad was so mad. Louis still says it was a very good Batman, but he still spent a few days in his bedroom grounded.

Dad was annoyed because he had just spent the best part of the day painting Louis's room and all that effort was wasted.

A few nights later at tea, Louis said to Dad then to Mom then to me,

"My painting is better than yours, Dad. I stayed inside the lines, and I did not get any paint on the door or the window."

Everybody just laughed except Dad. He just shook his head and said, "There's no winning with you, young man, is there? I had to paint that room a second time because of you and your Batman."

Louis did not even look up. He knew he had won that one for now. So he was going to quit while he was ahead.

All Mom said was, "Louis, don't be cheeky."

"Me, cheeky, Mom? Never. Truthful, yes, but cheeky? No, never."

"Louis, don't answer your Mom back."

"I wasn't."

"That's it, lad, one more word out of you."

"Okay, I will just sit here and stay quiet."

"Yes, we'll make sure you do."

"I will."

"Louis, stop while you're ahead."

"I did."

"Right, go to your room."

"Right, I will."

"Go."

"Go, Louis, before you push your Dad too far."

"I'm going." Louis jumped up from the table, knocking over the pot of tea across the table.

Dad jumped up.

Louis ran to his room, calling back, "Night."

Dad sat back down.

"Someday, he is going to go too far."

It was always the same; Louis would have the last word.

And get away with it.

Tazmaz and Malgit

Tazmaz was in the fields overseeing the Earth Keepers doing their work. They were finding it harder and harder to replenish the lands. Life had been drained out of the trees and the plants so many times there seems to be no will left in the land.

One of the Earth Keepers approached Tazmaz. "We have done all we can here, it's now up to the land to do the rest."

"Okay," said Tazmaz, "let's move on to the next field. We are behind, we have to get more done today."

The Earth Keeper turned to go but stopped. "It's Malgit."

Malgit's name travelled the length of the field faster than the wind.

All the Earth Keepers stopped working and just stood watching the Taker approach Tazmaz.

"Get on with your work," said Tazmaz.

Tazmaz looked at Malgit as he approached. *This can't be good*, he thought to himself, *the bringer of bad news.*

Malgit stopped in front of Tazmaz.

Malgit was almost twice the height of Tazmaz but only half the weight. Malgit looked so skinny, and he looked starved.

"Hello, my old friend," said Malgit.

"You did not come all this way to say hello to me?"

"No, I did not. Things are not right, I can smell it."

"Yes," said Tazmaz, "things are not right. You are in our lands, and you're not welcome. You do nothing, you kill our land, you are not wanted here. Why don't you go back to your own land where you belong?"

"Remember, you are only here, Tazmaz, because I allow it. For no other reason, you are in no position to ask or to tell me anything. You are only here to do as I bid when I tell you and answer the questions that I ask you."

"Someday we will rid our land of you and your people," said Tazmaz.

"Be careful you do not overstep yourself, Tazmaz, and don't try my patience because, Tazmaz, patience is not something I have much these days."

"Why are you here?" asked Tazmaz, changing the subject and knowing quite well Malgit's short temper and his power was a lot stronger than his.

"I decided to see how my workers are," said Malgit.

"We are well if we are left alone to do our work."

"Then tell me why there's a strong smell of unrest," said Malgit.

Malgit stared at Tazmaz for a long time.

Tazmaz could feel the Taker's stare go right through his very soul.

"I am very busy," said Tazmaz. "Is there anything else you want?"

"You are busy when I say you're busy," said Malgit. "Now tell me why things are not as they should be," said Malgit.

"Well, Malgit, if you know so much, why are you asking me these questions?"

Before Tazmaz could blink, Malgit had a grip on his throat.

Tazmaz started to feel dizzy then tired. He knew now what was happening to him. Malgit was draining the life from his very body, and everything was going black.

Malgit had a grip on Tazmaz's neck; he started to draw the force from within Tazmaz to his own body.

Yes, it felt good. He could feel his body being replenished, the strength from Tazmaz pouring into his own body. He could feel the power.

Tazmaz entered the world of darkness.

Malgit tossed the shell of Tazmaz to one side.

Malgit look around. There were seventy/eighty Earth Keepers standing, looking, not saying anything, fear and shock on their faces after seeing what had just happened to their leader.

"Get back to work," roared Malgit, "or you will suffer the same fate as him!" He pointed to the shell of Tazmaz lying on the ground.

The Earth Keepers started to move away.

Malgit headed off in the direction of the blue forest.

The Earth Keepers watched as Malgit headed off into the forest.

As soon as Malgit was out of sight, the Earth Keepers went over to where Tazmaz lay. They picked up his lifeless body, and they carried his body back to their cave. They entered their cave placing Tazmaz's body on a bed of straw beside the fire. One of the Earth Keepers took a bag from under a cluster of stones beside the table of stones at the wall. He went back over to Tazmaz and placed the bag on Tazmaz's chest. All the Earth Keepers sat around the body of their leader. No one said anything. They watched the bag; they sat for hours. Nothing happened, but still they sat watching. After a long time, there was a small light coming from inside the bag. It was hardly visible, but it was there. It shone through the bag, the Earth Keepers did not move. They stayed watching the bag. Slowly, over a long time, the light started to get brighter. The Earth Keepers, all except three, got up and went to rest. The three Earth Keepers stayed where they were, still watching the bag. They would stay there as long as required, even if it meant they would die sitting in that spot. They were chosen to do this, for they were the healers. They were the ones that made up the bags of crystals, one for each different sickness, and they were the ones that would travel to the Vox to acquire the crystals that they needed. And when one of the Earth Keepers was sick, they would place the crystals on the sick Earth Keeper and sit and watch. These three Earth Keepers did not work in the fields. They were responsible for all the clans of Earth Keepers. They would not eat or drink while they were healing, not till the Earth Keeper got well or died. Then and only then would they break their fasting.

They have been trained for this from birth.

The Beginning

"Now that we have had some rest and food," said Taz, "I think it's time for us to move on."

"Okay," said Sarah, "which way, and where are we going?"

"North," said Sko.

"Yes," said Taz, "to the border of the blue forest and the swamplands."

"To meet the wise man," said Sarah.

"Yes," said Taz. "So shall we get going? Time is not on our side."

All five got up and headed toward the edge of the blue forest.

Sarah looked around. This was not like the Glen. There were no flies bouncing off your face, and the trees were very close together, and with everything black, it was weird. Sarah looked up at the sky. Between the trees, the sky was still the same as when she had got here first: a dark, dirty gray like before a winter's storm. It was hard to tell the difference between day and night, and it was very warm.

Oh, what I would give to have a nice, hot bubble bath right now. She looked back at the Earth Keepers; they did not talk when they were moving.

They had travelled for a long while. When they came to a clearing in the forest, it was a small clearing, and it was safe.

"We will stop here for a rest and some food," said Taz.

"At last, I don't suppose there's a shower around here anywhere."

"A what?" asked Sko.

"A shower."

"What's a shower, Sarah?"

"Oh, nothing, Sko. It's just me being funny."

Sko just nodded. He didn't understand a word that Sarah was saying, a shower?

All five sat in a circle; they ate what food they had left.

"Beyond them trees is the swamp," said Mitz to Sarah.

"Just over there?" Sarah pointed at the trees to her right.

"Yes," said Sko.

"So we haven't got far to go now," said Sarah.

"Our journey is only about to begin. We haven't got too far to go, but this is the most dangerous part of the journey," said Taz.

"We are almost where we are supposed to be, but this is only the real start of the journey. We have to cross the swamp to the wise man's lands now, and for this part of the journey, we will need help. So now we must get started," said Taz.

"Help from who?" asked Sarah.

"You will have to wait and see. Now if everybody is finished, I think it best that we start on the rest of this journey."

All five got up and got themselves ready and started to head out of the clearing and back into the trees.

They were all heading toward the swamplands and hoping to meet up with the wise man, and maybe he could help them to complete their task.

The Roar

Malgit headed into the trees.

"Fools, all of them, if they think they can hide things from me. I know there's something amiss here. As for that Tazmaz standing up to me in front of his clan, well, they know now who rules these lands."

Malgit stopped and let out a loud roar and a second roar and waited.

Within minutes, Takers from all around merged on Malgit's space.

"Go search every inch of these woods from here to the blue forest. If you find any Earth Keepers, kill them. If you find any strangers, bring them to me. If you find any strangers and hurt them in any way, I will deal with you. Now go and get every Taker you find to help. I want these woods searched now before another cycle starts. And send word back to the black forest and tell the Takers there to look for any strangers. And if they find any, they are not to go near them, but they are to inform me where they are. Do you understand? Now go."

Malgit decided to search some of the woods himself.

But first there was something he must do; he must go to the swamplands and try to see the wise man, for he would know what is going on in these lands.

But he would not take kindly to a visit from Malgit.

They were not the best of friends, not since his last visit.

And the creatures he has guarding his lands are too strong for him to challenge on his own.

So I will have to be very tactful on how I deal with this.

He had made a promise to the wise man when the thorn went missing, and he and his people entered the lands of the Earth Keepers.

He promised not to harm the Earth Keepers.

And he did not harm any of them, but what his people did was not his fault. But the wise man would hold him responsible for any harm that came to the Earth Keepers.

Except for Tazmaz, but the wise man would not know of this yet, or would he?

And if he did, he was sure to blame me. He would blame me anyway for any harm that had fallen on the Earth Keepers, and he would make me pay for it somehow. And the wise man had the power to do just that.

Malgit started on his journey, knowing that this journey could mean the difference between life and death to him. But he had no choice, he had to stop whatever was going on, leader or no leader. He knew his fate. If his own turned on him, a slow and painful death at the hands of his own people.

He had seen one of the leaders put to death this way before; this was not for him. He had watched before as one of the leaders failed to keep control, and he watched as he was taken by the Takers and secured to a tree in the Clickers' lands. He watched as the Clickers picked and picked at him till he was only scrap. It took three cycles for him to die. No, that was not for him. He would not lose control, not for any reason no matter what the cost. He would control them any way he could, even with fear if he had to. And any Taker that crossed him would pay a dear price, and that was death in front of the Takers at Malgit's hand. That would be a lesson for them to learn and remember for a long time.

The Smell

Angela and Louis came to the edge of the forest. In front of them was what looked like muck or dried bog.

"Ah, Annie, it smells like—"

"Don't say it," said Angela. "I know what it smells like," she cut Louis in midsentence. "I have been here before."

"I know," said Louis. "But it's a real bad smell, you can't expect me to stay here with that smell. It's making me sick."

"You will get used to it. We have to cross that," said Angela.

"No way. I am not crossing that for nobody," said Louis.

"Well then, you will be left behind."

"Well now, that might not be a bad idea."

"Well, we have to wait here for now, so we may as well have something to eat," said Angela.

"I can't eat with that smell. I think I am going to vomit," said Louis.

"Don't you dare," said Angela, "or there will be hell to pay."

"I can't help it. I have never smelled anything as bad as that before."

"Try not to think about it and eat something."

"But, Annie, that smell is worse than, than anything I have ever smelled. It's even worse than Dad's fa—"

"Louis," Angela cut him, "I told you before, and it's the last time I will tell you, keep your comments to yourself."

"But, Annie, I can't eat with that smell."

Before Angela could say anything, they could hear the roar not once but twice.

"That's not a good sign, there is only one thing that can roar like that, and that's Malgit. And that roar is for a reason."

"What? A maggot? A maggot can't roar like that."

"Louis, sometimes you are beyond yourself. It's not a maggot. It's Malgit, the leader of the Takers."

"Okay, Malgit, maggot. It sounds the same, so what's a Malgit?"

"It's not a what, it's a who," said Angela. "He is the leader of the Takers, a nasty piece of work. And we don't want to meet him. Not now, not ever."

"Why not?" asked Louis.

"Because he is most likely the cause of all that's happened here, and he would kill you as quick as he would look at you. Now let's just sit here for a while and try to eat something."

"Eat what, Annie? I wish I had some of the bars. I left them all with Steve. Now them I could try to eat, you know, Annie. I would force myself."

"Yes, I bet you could. Now quiet, child, and eat."

Annie gave Louis some berries.

"Try these, they're quite good."

"Have you any McDonald's, now that I can eat, smell or no smell."

"I am really very sorry, Louis, but if you want to wait a little while, I can get you a McDonald's."

"Can you? Now that would be very nice. But how can you get McDonald's out here?"

Annie looked up at Louis.

"Ha-ha, very funny. That's one for you, Annie, and I still say it smells like Dad's—"

"Louis, eat your food, and no more smart remarks, okay?"

Louis knew how far he could push Annie, and she was almost at her limit now. Louis also knew when to back off. If Annie was this serious, then there must be a lot of trouble because it usually takes a lot to put Annie on the edge. The last time Louis saw Annie like this was when her cat died. There was no use talking to her for days, everybody was to blame. But she calmed down later on.

"Okay, Annie, I will try. Are they up berries, Annie?"

"Up berries? What are you talking about? They're just berries."

"Oh, I thought they were up berries."

"Up berries, I never heard of them. What's up berries?"

"They're the ones that when you eat them they come back up."

"Now we are even, Louis."

Louis had a smug grin on his face.

You have to get up early to catch me, he thought to himself.

The Meeting

Sarah and the Earth Keepers were walking toward the light.

"That's sunshine," said Sarah.

"Yes," said Taz, "it won't be long now till we reach the end of the forest."

"Oh, what's that horrid smell?" asked Sarah.

"That's the smell of the swamp," said Sko.

"The swamp?" asked Sarah.

"Yes," said Taz.

From behind them, they could hear the roar and the second roar.

"What's that?" asked Sarah.

The four Earth Keepers looked at each other.

Sarah thought she could see fear on their faces. No, she knew she could see fear on their faces.

They started to talk between themselves.

"That's rude to not include everyone. If it's something important, you should include me in the conversation as well," said Sarah.

"It's Malgit," said Sko, "and he's angry, and he's not far away."

"Yes," said Taz, "and he's on his way here. This is not a good sign. He must have found out what we are trying to do."

"So?" said Sarah.

"If he knows that we are trying to replace the fifth thorn, he will kill us and everything and everyone that helps us."

They started to walk again toward the light.

"We will have to move faster," said Taz.

"We will have to stay ahead of Malgit no matter what."

As they came to the clearing, they saw someone up ahead—no, two someones.

"Wait," said Taz. "This does not look good."

Sarah looked.

"I don't believe it." She called out Louis's and Angela's names,

Angela was just about to eat when, from just inside the tree line, she heard their names being called. "Louis, Angela."

She turned at the same time as Louis, looking toward the tree line.

Sarah came running out of the trees.

"Louis, Annie." Sarah was never so happy in her life to see them.

Louis jumped up and ran toward Sarah.

They met halfway, hugging each other.

"Hay, where's Steven? Is he not with you? You're never going to guess where I have been and what I done. And how come you and Annie are here?" asked Sarah.

"I don't know,' said Louis. "I touched her, and the witch brought me here. Do you smell that? It's worst than my Dad, and Steven is back in the camp waiting for Annie and me."

"Ah, she's not a witch, and yes, I can get the smell," said Sarah.

"Well, what is she then?" asked Louis.

"You have to understand this place to understand Annie. I want you to meet some of my new friends."

"Holy cow, what they are?" Louis said, pointing at the Earth Keepers.

"They're Earth Keepers," said Sarah.

Taz came over to Sarah. "We have to keep going."

"What did he say?" asked Louis.

"Oh, you don't understand them, do you?"

"No, do you?" asked Louis.

"Yes," said Sarah.

"And so do I," said Angela.

"Hello, Taz," said Angela. "And how are you?"

"I am fine, and how are you, gatekeeper?"

"Gatekeeper? You, Annie, you're the gatekeeper?"

"Yes, Sarah. I am good. Thank you for looking after Sarah."

"You're welcome. Here, drink this," said Taz.

"What did he say?"

"Drink this," said Sarah.

"What is it? Do I have to drink it? Does it smell?"

"Yes, you do have to drink it," said Sarah. "And no, it does not smell."

Louis took a swig from the bottle.

"How is it?" asked Taz.

"Grand," said Louis. "Hay, I can understand him. I know what he's saying. This is great. Can I have some for my dad so I can understand what he is saying sometimes?"

"Well, that's just dandy," said Angela. "So now we all understand each other, can we go on now? We have no time for family reunions."

"Yes," said Sko, "this is not a safe place to be at now."

They all moved to the edge of the swamp.

"What now?" asked Louis.

"We have to cross the swamp," said Angela.

"No way," said Louis, "not a hope. I am not stepping into that. I don't care who says what. It looks like what the cows left after a party, and if I have to stay here on my own, then so be it. But there's no way I am going near that, and I mean no way ever."

Miz stepped to the edge of the swamp. He took a small piece of wood from his pouch. It looked like a flute or a tin whistle. He put it into his mouth and blew on it, but there was no sound from it.

Louis looked at Sarah and made a circular motion with his finger at the side of his head.

"Nuts, totally gone like her." He pointed to Angela.

Sarah looked at Louis then at Angela then at Miz.

"What's he doing?" she asked.

"Calling the mudworm," said Miz.

"The what?" asked Louis.

"Wait and watch."

Taz looked at the edge of the swamp, everybody else started to look.

The mud started to ripple about thirty feet out.

"Look," said Louis.

"What?" said Sarah.

"Look over there," said Louis, just as their heads started to appear above the mud.

"This is our ride across the mud to the wise man," said Miz.

"Annie."

"Thank you, Miz," said Angela.

"Annie."

"You are welcome," said Miz.

"Annie."

"Yes, Louis?"

"Do we have to go on them? They look like snails."

"Yes, Louis." Louis looked at Sarah and back at Angela.

"Oh, nice one, Annie," said Louis. "I knew I could trust you to manage to get us on that sh—"

Angela gave Louis a stern look.

The creatures drew closer to the edge. They looked like snails but with two shells.

"We are going on them across that sh—"

"Louis," interrupted Angela, "we don't need your views. There is a lot more serious things going on here, and we have to deal with them. There's no time for your sulking. Now keep your views to yourself and let's get on with what we have to do here. Otherwise, you can stay here and face Malgit when he arrives. Now get on the mudworm and keep your mouth shut."

Louis looked at Sarah and made a funny face behind Annie's back.

It took Sarah all she had to stop from laughing.

When Louis turned back around, Annie was looking at him.

"Young man, I am sick and tired of talking to you. Now it seems you have a choice. You can do as you're told, or you can stay here, and trust me, when you see what's coming this way, you won't want to be here. And by that time, it will be too late to come with us. Now make up your mind. What's it to be?"

"Sorry, Annie, I am going to do as I am told." He turned to Sarah and winked at her.

"Right so."

"Right, so I might as well be in the sh—"

"Louis."

"Sorry, Annie."

The Mudworm
___

"They're big," said Sarah.

"Yes, child, now come on," said Angela, "we have to get to the very edge."

They all stood on the edge, waiting for the mudworm to come close to the edge so they could get on their backs.

"What are they?" asked Louis.

"They are the mudworms," said Taz.

As the mudworm drew closer, Miz turned to Sko. "Do you hear that?" Sko's ears stood up. "Yes."

"What?" asked Angela. "What did you hear?"

"It's the Clickers, and there is a lot of them. Maybe two or three swarms, or maybe more, and by the sound of them, they are heading this way."

"That's not good," said Angela. "We need to run for cover."

"What's not good?" asked Louis.

"Never mind, child. But we have to make a choice. Do we cross the swamp, or do we go back to the forest?" said Angela.

"We can't go back to the forest. We all heard Malgit. He is on his way here, and the mudworm won't come back again," said Taz.

"Well, it likes we have no choice," said Sarah as she spoke. A swarm of Clickers came over the tree line. The noise was deafening; a second swarm came from the opposite direction.

"Run," said Sko. Sko lead. He ran toward the mudworm. With one bounce, he was on the back of one of them. Sko turned and shouted, "Come on, hurry!"

Louis was next, followed by Miz then Wapz then Sarah and then Angela.

Taz was running when, out of the sky, a Clicker swooped, grabbing on to Taz and taking off into the sky.

Sarah could see the shocked look on Taz's face.

"No!" roared Sarah, "no no!" But before anyone could say anything, the Clicker and Taz disappeared over the trees. The rest of the swarm seemed to be busy attacking something else in the distance.

The mudworm backed out into the swamp and headed off in the opposite direction away from the forest and into the swamp.

The Clickers paid no attention to them. They were far too busy with something else.

Sarah was uncontrollable. She sobbed and sobbed. Louis put his arm around Sarah; he did not say anything, for once Louis was lost for words.

"It's not fair. This is a mean place, and I want to go home. I am sick of all this. I only wanted to go on holidays and have some fun. It's not fair."

"It's going to be all right," said Angela.

"I don't care about them and their stupid thorn. This has nothing to do with me, and I just want to go home."

The three Earth Keepers just sat there; they said nothing.

They felt helpless and lost, it was hard for them to lose one of their own. But it was something they were getting used to lately.

Sarah asked in a low voice between sobs, "Is there nothing anybody can do for Taz? Please we have to be able to do something for him. We just can't sit here and do nothing."

Wapz looked at Sarah and shook his head. "We are sorry, Sarah, but we each promised to protect you with our lives, to make sure you reach the wise man's safe. You getting to the wise man is more important than anything."

Sarah thought she could see tears in Wapz's eyes.

Wapz was remembering his close call with the Clickers and how Sarah had helped him. If weren't for her, he would not be here today. He knew he was very lucky. And how Taz healed his wounds.

He felt so sad and helpless.

Wapz reached out for Sarah's hand.

Sarah looked at Wapz; Wapz put out his hand. Sarah held Wapz's hand. "But it's not fair."

Angela looked on, thinking, *Ah, that poor child. This is very hard on her.* Angela wanted to hug her, but other things were on her mind.

Angela felt uneasy; things were very quiet.

Angela remembered the last time she was here in the swamp; things were a lot more active. There was more life, but there was nothing now, except the mudworm.

Angela looked ahead, but she could see nothing. With the mist from the swamp and the dark clouds, the couple of seconds of sunshine had disappeared. It was pitch black.

Angela shook, not with the cold but with uneasiness.

Things felt different; things were out of place.

"Are you okay, Annie?" asked Louis.

"Yes, child. Just a little cold, thank you."

"Oh, okay," said Louis. Louis looked at Sarah.

Annie pulled her cardigan tight around her.

Something is different, but Annie did not know what.

"Are you sure you're okay, Annie?" asked Sarah.

"Yes, child."

Sarah and Louis looked at each other; they had never seen Annie act so odd before. She looked like she was a million miles away.

Maybe it's just me, Angela thought to herself, *but there is something evil and mean out there. I can feel it in my bones, and whatever it is, it's not far away. The only other things in the swamp were the Sinkers, a mean creature about ten feet long.*

They would come from under you and stick to you. Once stuck, there was no way to get free, and then they would sink back under the mud. After that, no one knew what happened as no one or nothing ever came back. But they don't attack the mudworm. Why I don't know. Maybe it's just me, thought Angela, *but there seems to be a lot of changes around here lately.*

And I am not sure why. Even the mud flies were missing, and that's a first because there was always millions of them. They would be in your mouth, your face, and stick to your hair. But not one.

Sarah looked at Annie's face. She could see that Annie was worried. Something was very wrong; she had never seen Annie look this troubled before.

"Are you sure you're all right, Annie?"

"Yes, child."

Sarah looked back at Louis. She shook her head.

Louis put his hand up. He knew by Annie's face there was something very wrong.

The Takers

Angela just shook her head. This has to get better.

The mudworm just slid across the swamp.

Nobody was in shape to speak.

They just sat on the mudworm as they slid deeper into the swamp.

"Ah, I can't take any more of that smell," said Louis.

"What are you going to do, get off and walk?" said Angela.

"Ha-ha, funny," said Louis, "you're so full of wit."

"Be quiet," said Sko. "I can hear something."

"What?" asked Sarah.

"Quiet," said Angela.

"Look," said Sko. "Takers coming through the trees."

"I knew my feelings were not wrong. They know that we are here. And if they know, so does Malgit."

"Does this get any better?" asked Louis.

"Not from here on in," said Angela.

"Between the maggots and the smell, what a way to spend a Sunday."

"Do you always have to be so smart?" said Sarah.

"Don't forget, it's not my fault we are all here," said Louis.

"At least they can't enter the swamp," said Miz.

"Who?" said Sarah.

"The Takers," said Miz.

"Can they not?" said Louis. "Well, what's that?" he said, pointing toward the mud's edge.

They all turned to look at where Louis was pointing.

The Takers were putting their hands into the mud. As they did, the mud started to harden.

"What are they doing?" asked Sarah.

"They are putting the life they have drained back into the swamp, making the ground hard so that it can support life so they can use it to walk on," said Angela.

They all watched.

The Takers were about twelve feet out into the swamp on hard ground just under halfway to where Angela, Sarah, Louis, and the Earth Keepers were.

"This is not good," said Angela. "At the speed they are working, they will be here very quick."

Two Takers would kneel on the ground, putting their hands into the mud. Within seconds, two more would move in front of them and do the same.

The mudworm was moving at half the speed of the Takers.

The Takers were now over halfway to Angela.

"Do something, Annie," said Louis.

"I am sorry, child, but there is nothing I can do."

"Can you do anything?" Louis asked the Earth Keepers.

They all shook their head.

The Takers were now only a foot away from the mudworm with Angela and crew on its back.

Sarah felt a heat on her chest.

Looking down, she saw the pouch with the crystal in it. The crystal was warm and was starting to glow.

Looking back at the Takers, Sarah could see the biggest, ugliest thing; it was walking on the hard ground toward Sarah only a foot away.

Sarah took the crystal out of the pouch and held it in her right hand close to her chest.

Sarah then put her hand into the mud.

The crystal began to give out a very bright light.

The mud that had gone hard nearest the mudworm started to go soft again.

The big, ugly-looking thing stopped. He looked at the mud then at Sarah. It took a few seconds for him to realize what was happening.

"Go back," he roared at the Takers. He himself turned and ran back to the swamp's edge.

Most of the Takers were not fast enough. They sank into the mud.

As they did, black things came up out of the mud and started to roll. The Takers started to stick to the back of the creatures. As soon as they did, the creatures disappeared under the mud.

Angela and Louis and the three Earth Keepers looked on in shock.

Louis turned to Angela. "Close your mouth, Annie."

Angela looked at Louis and laughed, payback.

Angela hugged Sarah and said, "Yes, child, you are the one."

"The one what?" asked Sarah.

"Later, child," said Angela.

The three Earth Keepers bowed to Sarah.

"Thank you," all three said together.

"You are all more than welcome," said Sarah.

They all sat quietly on the back of the mudworm as it slowly advanced forward in the mud to the wise man.

Leaving Malgit on the edge of the swamp.

All the Takers in the mud had now disappeared.

The Clickers Attack

The Takers were coming to the edge of the forest.

They knew they were close to the strangers. They could smell them.

They also knew that Malgit was close behind them.

As they were coming to the forest edge, they could hear the clicking noise. Coming from above them, the noise was everywhere.

They came to a clearing in the forest, and from out of nowhere, the sky was black with Clickers.

The Clickers swooped down on the Takers, picking them off one by one and taking back to the skies.

The Takers were easy pickings for the Clickers.

The Clickers were out in force as they had a lot of young to feed.

And when they were in flight, nothing and no one was safe.

Over four hundred Takers had entered the clearing, less than one hundred made it to safety.

But their fear of Malgit was greater than their fear of the Clickers, so they just kept going into the clearing in spite of the dangers that waited there for them.

Malgit arrived just as the Clickers were leaving.

He could see the Clickers with the Takers in their claws.

The Takers were unable to use their powers on the Clickers.

Malgit moved on across the clearing into the trees, and as Malgit was coming out of the trees to the swamp, he could see the strangers on the back of a mudworm, leaving the edge of the swamp.

Malgit was furious.

"Get them," he ordered.

He ordered the Takers to line up in twos and use their powers on the mud to make the mud hard.

The Takers lined up in twos.

Two Takers put their hands on to the mud.

The mud was hard in seconds.

Two more went in front of the first two and did the same and so on till Malgit was able to walk on the mud.

Malgit walked across the hard mud. He was getting closer to the mud worm; he would have the strangers very quickly.

Malgit watched from about twelve feet the young female on the back of the mudworm take something from a pouch around her neck. She placed it into her right hand and then placed her hand into the mud.

Malgit watched as the thing shone.

Crystals, how did she get a crystal? The Vox, that is the only way she would get one.

The mud started to get soft again.

Malgit stopped.

"No, not now, not when I am so close. Harder!" he roared at the Takers.

But their best effort was just not enough against the power of the crystal. The crystal was working twenty/thirty times faster than the Takers' best efforts. They had no chance.

Malgit had no choice but to turn and return to the swamp's edge and watch as his Takers vanished into the mud.

At the swamp's edge, Malgit watched the mudworm slowly move on out into the swamp with the strangers on its back.

So close and yet so far. Enjoy your freedom for now.

But our paths will cross again soon, and when they do, you will not get away so easy, and I promise you will pay for today.

Malgit stood at the swamp's edge, watching the mudworm vanish into the mist.

Malgit knew of another way across the swamp. But it would cost him a lot of his people to go that way.

It had cost him a lot of his people today between the Clickers and the mud; he would have to be careful from here on in.

It meant he would have to go through the homelands of the Clickers, and that is one thing that the Clickers don't like—strangers in their homeland. Today's losses would be nothing to the losses that they would occur in the Clickers' lands.

But Malgit had no choice now. If he gave up now, the Takers would turn on him.

Malgit instructed the Takers to follow him.

As he started walking along the swamp's edge to the homeland of the Clickers, he could use the safe path in the swamp. But the dangers there were greater than taking the chance in the land of the Clickers.

There was a lot of unrest among the Takers, for they knew that Malgit was heading toward the Clickers' lands, and they did not like it one bit.

Malgit could hear the murmurs from behind him. But getting the strangers was most important; he would deal with the troublemakers later.

The Challenge

Malgit was in a foul humor.

"They have got away from me and all the powers my troops have. Not one of them could catch the strangers."

Malgit had thirty thousand Takers in the Earth Keepers' land, and he had sent a roar to summon them all to the task at hand: to catch the strangers. Not one of the thirty thousand could do this. Per usual, he had to take personal supervision over everything that was important.

But they would pay for his time, and the Takers would pay more dearly for failing him. This is one time too many that the Takers had let him down. *But the journey at hand would teach them not to fail me again. They would learn to follow my instruction, or they would pay dearly, and they would pay in the land of the Clickers.*

Malgit would take great pleasure in catching the strangers. He intended to draw every ounce of life from them. Slowly, there would be nothing quick about their end, not like Tazmaz's. It would not be quick,

He would make them pay; he would end their lives over cycles. Yes, a little each cycle, he would make them last a long time. Yes, nothing would be quick for them.

He looked behind to see the Takers had stopped.

Malgit turned and faced them.

"I told you to keep up, now move."

None of the Takers moved, but from the mass of Takers, one stepped forward.

Malgit walked back to this single Taker till he was within feet from him.

Malgit studied this Taker. He was almost as big as Malgit. Malgit knew this was going to be a challenge to the leadership.

"Kaymoe, get back into the ranks."

Kaymoe did not move.

"Is there something wrong with you?"

"Yes, Malgit, I have decided that you are not fit to be in charge of the Takers anymore. And I will now give you the chance to step down and bow to me and join the ranks of the Takers."

"Well, let me see. You are taking the leadership," said Malgit, "and is this decision from of all of you?"

Malgit looked at the Takers.

None of the Takers answered.

"I ask you again, is this decision from of all of you?"

Kaymoe turned to look at the Takers. As he turned back to face Malgit, he felt Malgit's grip on his throat.

Kaymoe was every bit as fast. He grabbed Malgit by the throat.

Malgit's grip tightened around Kaymoe's throat.

Kaymoe pushed forward, knocking Malgit off balance.

Malgit stumbled and fell.

Kaymoe fell with Malgit landing on top of him. Malgit lost his grip on Kaymoe, but Kaymoe's grip was even tighter on Malgit's throat than before.

Kaymoe could feel the power going into his body from Malgit.

Malgit began to feel weak. He knew that Kaymoe had the upper hand. Malgit had to break Kaymoe's grip.

With every ounce of strength in his body, he made a last effort to pry Kaymoe's grip from his throat, but the grip was to strong.

Malgit started to weaken; he could see the darkness coming.

With one last try, he grabbed Kaymoe's head and bit his ear.

Kaymoe screamed with pain and let go the grip he had on Malgit.

That was the break Malgit was waiting for. Malgit gripped Kaymoe's throat and squeezed. Yes, he could feel the power and the strength returning to his body. He was getting stronger.

He could feel Kaymoe's body buckle and weaken. Within seconds, it was all over. Kaymoe was no more.

Malgit stood erect and roared a long roar, a roar of victory.

All the Takers fell to the ground. They knew their chance to rid themselves of Malgit was gone. Their fear of Malgit had now grown stronger, and Malgit knew this.

Malgit stood and looked at the Takers. He would find out who was responsible for this, but that will wait. He had more important things to do first. And that was to get the strangers.

Malgit had to plan on how to get into the Clickers' homeland and out as fast as possible with the minimum loss of life, and the best time for this would be at night when the Clickers are resting, and the young are asleep. Even at night, this was not going to be an easy task.

Malgit's work was cut out for him, and on top of all this, there was unrest among the Takers. Malgit was no fool. He knew there were three more Takers with the power to make a challenge to his leadership. Malgit had to be very careful on how he handled things.

Malgit continued on with his journey as if nothing had happened.

"Follow me," he called to the Takers.

After thirty steps, Malgit knew the Takers were following him.

Their fear was too great not to.

Good, thought Malgit, *time to get on with the business at hand.*

Malgit carried on. Sure, he had put a stop to any more attempts of his leadership.

Malgit did not hear the two Takers down at the back.

If he did, he would have watched his back more closely.

The two Takers had decided to join forces and take power from Malgit.

These two Takers were from the same clan as Kaymoe, and they were not happy with the way Malgit was wasting the Taker's lives to fulfill his own gains. They would watch and wait for the moment to strike.

This would be soon, and they would move fast and swift.

Trouble

Angela, Sarah, Louis, and the Earth Keepers were well on their way.

"This place still smells," said Louis, holding his nose.

"Well, we will see what we can do about that for you," said Angela.

"Really?" asked Louis.

Sarah laughed at Louis. "You know, sometimes you can be so thick."

"I'm not thick," said Louis, looking upset and offended.

"We are in the middle of a swamp that smells, and you think Annie can do something about the smell," said Sarah.

Before anybody could say anything, there was a roar stronger than any roar they heard before, a roar that would travel the length of Mogieland.

Annie looked at the Earth Keepers.

And they looked at Annie.

"Trouble?" asked Annie.

"Yes," said Sko, "big trouble for us."

"Yes," said Annie, "I thought that was what that meant."

"Yes," said Sko, "it sounds like Malgit has won a leadership challenge. And now there is no power in these lands to stop him."

"No powers, except maybe the wise man's," said Angela.

"Maybe, or maybe not. We will have to wait and see what the wise man says."

They looked in front of them; there was nothing to see except mist.

The mist was everywhere; they could not see their hand in front of them.

"There could be anybody or anything out there, and we would not know till they were on top of us. They could kill us, and nobody would ever know."

"Do you know what I think?"

"No, Louis, and we don't want to know," said Sarah.

Before Louis could answer, the mudworm came to a stop.

"What's wrong now?" asked Louis, looking at Annie.

"Quiet," said Annie.

The mist started to thin out.

"Look," said Sarah, pointing directly in front of her.

"What?" said Louis, "I can't see anything."

"Yes, I can see it," said Sko.

"And I," said Miz.

"And I can see it too," said Angela.

"What? I can't see anything except mist," said Louis.

"The land, the lovely green lawn, and the flowers, and look, it's a house in the far distance. Come on, let's go," said Sarah.

"I still can't see anything."

"Look, Louis, over there."

"No, nothing, Sarah, except mist,"

"Let him hold your crystal," said Sko to Sarah.

Sarah took the crystal from around her neck and placed it in Louis's hand. Angela watched on.

The crystal started to glow.

"No, nothing," said Louis.

"Give it a chance," said Angela, "it will take a while to get through to someone as thick as you."

"You're not a bit funny."

Sarah started to laugh till Louis looked at her.

"Hay, I can see it now."

Louis jumped off the mudworm and onto the grass.

"Come on, you lot, what are you waiting for?"

Before anyone could utter a word, two big dog things, like Great Danes but with lion's heads and six legs, were upon them. Louis froze on the spot.

"Annie!" screamed Louis.

Everybody turned to look at Louis.

The Creatures

"Don't move!" screamed Sarah.

Louis was shaking; he could not move, not even talk.

One of these things walked up to Louis, putting his nose to Louis's face. It started to sniff Louis. After twenty or so seconds, it roared. Louis turned white.

The second creature walked to the mudworm and sat facing Angela.

Sarah and the Earth Keepers were rooted to the mudworm. They were terrified to even breathe.

Angela started to walk toward the grass.

Once on the grass, Angela walked over to the creature that was sitting in front of her. When she got to arm's length of the creature, she put her hand out. The creature got up and sniffed Angela's hand.

After a few seconds, the creature lay down and rolled over on his back. Angela started rubbing his belly.

"That's a good boy, Jack. How's Annie's baby?" The creature let out a little moan. "Ah, you big pussycat."

The second creature started to lick Louis.

"It's okay, Louis, you can rub her, and her name is Tess."

"Are you sure?"

Annie walked over to Tess.

"Who's a good girl?" And she started to lick Annie.

Annie turned to Sarah and the Earth Keepers.

"It's okay, they are friendly. You can come over."

Sarah and the Earth Keepers left the mudworm and came alongside Annie.

"Give him a rub, Sarah. Let him know you're friendly."

When Sarah put her hand out to rub Jack, Jack first sat then lay down. As soon as he was lying down, Tess walked over to Jack and lay beside him. Both were facing Sarah.

"That's odd," said Annie, "they have never done that before."

The two creatures rolled over on their backs.

Sarah started to rub Jack's belly.

"Have you been here before?" said Sarah.

"Yes," said Annie.

"You could have told us about these things," said Louis.

"And miss the look on your face? No way, it was worth all the money in the world to see that expression on your face," said Angela.

"Well, I don't think it was very funny, witch."

"What are they?" asked Sko.

"They are the guardians. They protect the wise man and the wise man's lands. Don't let them fool you, they can take down and rip apart a Taker or Clicker in seconds."

"For real, Annie?" asked Louis.

"For real," said Annie.

"That's cool. Can I take one home?"

"I don't think so."

Louis pulled a face behind Angela's back.

The Earth Keepers stayed behind Sarah. They were smaller than Jack and Tess and still afraid of them, and they were not taking any chances.

"Come on, babies," Angela said to Jack and Tess, "let's find your master."

Angela started across the lawn to the front was a pond, and beyond that was a group of trees. With Louis stuck to her side, they headed toward the pond and Jack and Tess behind her and with Sarah between them and the Earth Keepers following up.

Angela looked back at Sarah.

We have something special here, she thought to herself, *Jack and Tess are protecting Sarah. I wonder what the wise man will make of that.*

"Annie, can I ask you a question?" asked Louis.

"Of course you can, child."

"Are we ever going to get out of here alive?"

Angela laughed. "Of course we are, child, but we have a task to do first, and it's not going to be easy. So, my little man, you have to be brave and help Sarah as much as you can."

"Can you not help us?"

"No, child, this is as far as I can go."

"Why?"

"Well, child, I am the gatekeeper, and I am only allowed to bring people to and from the wise man. After that, I am helpless to do any more. Only you and Sarah can for fill the task. The wise man will only tell you what you must do, that is all. And the Earth Keepers were to protect you till you got to here. They can't go any farther."

"So we're pretty much on our own from here on in?"

"Yes, child, I am afraid very much so."

"Oh, that's just great."

"That's your destiny, child."

Sarah had gone ahead of the rest.

Angela was still talking to Louis when she noticed Jack's ears stand up, and both Jack and Tess froze on the spot, turning their heads to the left.

Sarah noticed this. "Jack, Tess, what's wrong?"

Jack growled.

"Sit, Jack, sit, Tess."

But both creatures stood, and both were growling.

"Annie," called Sarah.

"Something's wrong," said Annie.

Jack let out a roar and then stood growling.

Within minutes, five more creatures came charging across the field. They were the same as Jack and Tess. Before you could blink, they were beside Jack and Tess.

These five creatures were the offsprings of Jack and Tess.

All seven creatures took off, heading toward the small group of trees to the left.

They ran so fast. Within a second, they were only a blur.

"What's wrong, Annie?" asked Louis.

"I don't know, but it's not good. But whatever it is, they will deal with it, you can be sure of that."

The creatures were out of sight within seconds.

"Come on, kids, we have to move fast."

They all followed Angela.

They all headed toward the small pond. Behind the pond, there was a group of trees shaped like a horseshoe.

As they approached the pond, they could see Jack and Tess coming from their trees to the left, almost the same place that they had entered, and behind them were the five younger ones.

They had only been gone a few minutes.

Sarah called to Jack and Tess; they both came directly over to Sarah.

Tess sniffed Sarah and started to lick her hand.

Sarah noticed blood all around Tess's mouth and the same on all the other creatures. She said nothing.

Sarah rubbed Tess's head, and they started on their way again.

"Go to the right and head for that gap in the trees."

"We should be there in a few minutes, and, Sarah, they will have to wait there. They are not allowed into the gardens,"

"Why, Annie?" asked Sarah.

"It's not my rule, child. Anyway, they know they are not allowed into the gardens unless the wise man summons them."

As they entered the gap between the trees, Jack and Tess took off at speed back into the trees.

"Where are they going now?" asked Sarah.

"I don't know, but they are acting funny. They are never like this. But you can be sure they are on the scent of something."

"Could be dinner," said Louis. "Maybe they have seen a rabbit."

"Could be, but I don't think so. I think it's more important than that."

"What then, Annie?" asked Sarah.

"I don't know, but whatever it is, they will sort it out. Now we have to go, everybody head to the house. Once we are there, the wise man will explain everything to us, and you will be able to rest and have something to eat"—Annie looked at Louis—"and a wash."

"What about you, Annie?"

"I have things to do and places to be."

Annie looked at Louis. *He is a little pale*, she thought to herself. *It must have been the fright he got, meeting Jack and Tess. He will be okay as soon as he gets some food and some rest.* She looked at Sarah. *My, she is holding up well. She should be okay for the task that lies ahead of her. Well, I hope she will be. After all, she is the wise man's choice. I thought she was a little young, but I was outvoted. I hope this one time in my life, I was wrong.*

The Attack

A dozen Takers had come down south, heading to the land of the Earth Keepers. But somehow, when they were crossing the safe path in the swamp, they came across a green area of land. Happy with themselves on finding this place, they could now get some much-needed food. There was life everywhere. They entered the green area; they started to draw life from the trees and plants.

One of the Takers looked up from what he was doing only to see a load of creatures heading toward them at a very fast speed.

The Taker called out to the rest, "Look, something is coming."

Most of the Takers were too busy to look till it was too late.

The creatures were upon them before they could blink an eye.

The creatures attacked, showing no mercy, tearing the Takers apart limb by limb. Their attacks had to be planned, or they learned over the years the best way to cripple the enemy. They attacked each Taker, tearing the legs from them or taking their heads off. The first Taker stood up to look. As he did, the creature jumped over him. As the creature landed and turned, he dropped the head of the Taker, he had jumped over to the ground. The Takers' bodies fell into a heap, the creature had already taken the legs from the second Taker. Before the first Taker even knew what happened, their speed left the Takers helpless to do anything. Even if they could do anything, it would have been too little too late. One of the creatures would have been enough to take down the dozen Takers, but with seven of them, their work was finished within seconds. All that was left of the Takers were their bodies scattered all over the place. Not one was alive, all twelve had been taken apart and scattered around the place.

The creatures checked back over the bodies of the Takers to make sure they were dead. When they were happy that not one Taker remained alive, they all headed back toward the wise man's lands to protect the strangers who had just arrived. This was the wise man's wish. Jack sent two of them back to watch the gap into the wise man's lands.

The two young Tallis took up a position just inside the tree line where they could not be seen. They lay there and waited.

Malgit's Death

Malgit was now at the west side of the swamp, he had decided to take the long way around to the land of the Clickers. He also knew that there was a gap into the wise man's lands, somewhere along the safe path through the swamp, and this could save him a lot of time and a lot of his Takers where it was at its narrowest. If there was any place to enter the swamp, it was here. There was a safe path around here somewhere. This was the path he had used to cross from the black forest to the blue forest, and it passed very close to the wise man's home.

As Malgit came down the path, he stopped. Looking to his right across into a field that had color, he thought to himself, *This is the start of the wise man's lands*. Then Malgit noticed something. He studied it a little longer, it looked like bits of bodies. They were scattered all over the place. They were the remains of Takers. What could have done this? There must be ten or twelve Takers there. Malgit shook. Whatever it was, he did not want to meet up with it. There was one way to find out. Malgit called six of his men forward. "Go and collect the remains of the Takers in that field."

The Takers backed away when they saw what was in the field.

"Go," ordered Malgit.

The six Takers backed off into the main body.

Malgit's patience was getting very thin.

He picked some more of the Takers, but they refused to go.

Two Takers came from the ranks; they were as big as Malgit.

The first one stood close to Malgit, while the second walked behind Malgit.

"Why don't you go? Seems you're so worried."

Malgit studied the Taker and his position with the second one. Malgit knew he had no chance of beating the two of them.

Even though they were slightly smaller than him, there were two of them.

Malgit just looked at the two Takers.

Malgit crossed from the safe path to the green grass treading careful, for he knew whatever had taken down these Takers was strong and fast. As he approached the center of the remains, he never even saw them coming. Malgit dropped to the ground headless.

The Takers stood and watched the challenge. No one spoke, for they were all trying to hear what was been said.

They watched as Malgit walked into the green lands and over to where the remains of the Takers were. They watched as a blur passed Malgit, and his headless body dropped to the ground. None of them was sure what had happened.

They all stood shocked. They had heard stories of the protectors on the wise man's grounds, but no one had ever seen them.

Now they were confronted by two creatures they had never seen before. The creatures stood spaced about six foot apart, facing the Takers, watching. The creatures could not leave the green area.

They stood ready to pounce, watching, waiting for one or all the Takers to move forward.

Slowly the Takers started to back away, none of them wanted to confront these things.

With Malgit now gone, there were two leaders. They both looked at each other.

"We have to set the example."

They both roared, "Follow us," and they charged toward the creatures. About a hundred Takers followed.

The creatures roared.

Within seconds, the five other creatures were beside them.

The creatures waited till the Takers were almost upon them.

Then they pounced with lighting speed. Jack beheaded one of the leaders and then five more Takers. Tess took out the other leader. The rest came in behind Tess. Within five minutes, the Takers who charged the creatures were all dead, their bodies scattered in every direction.

Most of the Takers did not even see their attackers till it was too late.

The rest of the Takers fled in all directions, except into the green area where the creatures were standing together watching, waiting.

Some of the Takers ran off the safe path into the swamp. The Sinkers finished off the Takers in the swamp.

Some headed back the way they came; the rest just ran into the forest.

Louis

Sarah and the rest heard the cry, "Charge!"

"What's going on?" she asked Annie. "That sounds like a fight."

"Seems there is some business that the pets are taking care of."

"What business is that?"

"You will find out later, child, it's not for me to tell you. Now we have to keep moving, we are almost there."

"But, Annie, it's hard trying to get through these trees."

"I know, child, but do your best. It won't be for long."

"Why can't we just walk straight to the house? Why did we have to go the long way around? We could see the house from the swamp. Why did we have to go through the trees?"

Annie turned and looked at Louis, who was white.

"Are you all right, child?" she asked Louis.

"No, Annie, I don't feel well. I think I want to be sick, and everywhere hurts. If I could just stop for a while and rest or even sleep, I know I would be all right."

The smile vanished off Annie's face. "Child, try hold on. It's not far, and the wise man will look after you, and you can rest there."

"Okay."

He must be sick, that's not like Louis to be so quiet, she thought to herself, *even if it's only to call me a witch.* She was worried.

"Okay, kids and Earth Keepers, we must hurry. I think Louis has caught a bug in the swamp, and we have to get him to the wise man as quickly as possible."

"What's wrong with Louis, Annie?" asked Sarah.

"Oh, it's like flu. He should be okay when we get him to the wise man."

"Will the healing crystal help him?" asked Sko.

"No, I don't think so, and we don't have the time to stop. Thank you."

Angela was worried; Sarah could see it on her face.

Louis looked clammy and pale; he did not look like the Louis that Sarah knew. He really looked sick.

Before Sarah could ask if they had far to go, they came out of the trees. "Wow, look at that."

"Yes, child, we are on the wise man's land now."

Sarah just stood and looked; she had never seen anything like it before except in magazines or books. The grass was like a carpet, and you could smell all the flowers, not together but each one, at a time. And the rows of trees, there were apple, pear, plum, every type you could think of, even a banana tree. And over to the right was a small cottage, like the ones you would see in the country in the 1900s.

"This is paradise, Annie."

"Yes, it's quite nice. Now we must hurry. Louis does not look any better."

As Angela spoke, Louis collapsed to the ground.

"Oh, dear, he is sicker than I thought he was. We have to hurry."

The three Earth Keepers picked Louis off the ground.

"Now please hurry," said Angela. She had no sooner spoken the words, and the Earth Keepers were gone.

"They can move very fast," said Sarah.

"Yes," said Angela, "they can at that."

The three Earth Keepers were already outside the wise man's house before Angela finished what she was saying.

"Come on now, child, we have to catch up."

As they were leaving the fields of trees, Sarah could see the Earth Keepers enter the wise man's house with Louis.

"Will he be okay, Annie?"

"Yes, he should be now. Please hurry."

"Yes, Annie," Sarah said as she started to run.

"Wait, child, I am not as young as you."

They arrived at the wise man's house together.

The door was wide open, and Annie ran inside.

"Ah, hello," the wise man said, "Angela and Sarah, come on in and make yourselves comfortable. I will be with you in a second."

Sarah was rooted to the ground; she could not believe her eyes. She was in total shock; her mouth was open.

Malful

Most of the Takers had gathered in the field in the black forest. They had no leader, and with no leader, the Takers were lost. They needed a leader, someone who would give the orders for them to follow.

In the field were hundreds of Takers, if not thousands. In the middle of them was one Taker. He was a nothing, a nobody. He sat with the rest of the Takers. Mindless, he felt odd. Something was starting to happen to him; his body was starting to grow. He was stretching. As his body started to stretch, it brought pain, pain like he never felt before. He started to scream out.

The Taker next to him looked on; he did not know what was going on. All he knew was the Taker in front of him was starting to grow and change. Taker after Taker looked on. One of the older Takers that was watching shouted out, "Our new leader is being born."

All the Takers stood and watched as one Taker grew from three feet to four to five to six and on till he stood twelve feet tall. He looked around. He could see over all the Takers right down to the back. There were thousands of Takers there now watching, waiting for their first order.

The new leader looked at the crowds, not sure what to do or say. He called out in a loud voice,

"I AM MALFUL, I AM THE LEADER OF ALL THE LANDS AND TAKERS IN
THE LANDS. I NOW ORDER YOU ALL TO GO AND FIND ALL THE TAKERS

IN ALL THE LANDS AND BRING THEM BACK TO THE BLACK FOREST,
FOR THE TIME HAS COME TO RID THIS LAND OF ALL STRANGERS
AND THE WISE MAN AND HIS DEMONS THAT PROTECT HIM. THE
LANDS HE RULES OVER WILL BECOME OURS. NOW GO."

Every Taker started to move in every direction to follow the orders of their new leader, Malful.

The Instructions

Sarah was in shock. She was speaking, but nothing was coming out of her mouth.

"Take a deep breath, child."

Sarah took a deep breath as the tears rolled down her face.

"Nana" was all that came out of her mouth.

"Yes, Sarah bear, come on in." This was Nana's nickname for Sarah. She also called her cupcakes as she did with Louis.

It took Sarah a few seconds to get her limbs to move, but when she did, she wrapped both arms around her grandmother's neck and sobbed.

"Now, now, Sarah bear. Take a few deep breaths. Let's get you inside, and you can tell me everything that has happened to you."

"Yes, Nana, how is Louis?"

As Sarah went in the door of the cottage, Sarah could smell baking. She could see Louis on a big bed over to the left, looking around. There was a table in the middle of the room where the three Earth Keepers were eating. Behind them was a dresser full of jars.

"Nana, are you the wise man, and what's wrong with Louis?"

"Yes, Sarah bear, I am the wise person, and Louis is okay. He swallowed some of the muck in the swamp, but he will be sick for a little while. But he should be as right as rain in a few hours. Now come and sit down and have some pie and milk and tell me everything."

Sarah sat at the table, taking a mouthful of pie. She started to tell Nana everything that had happened to her. When she finished talking, she ate more pie.

"What's this, Nana? It's tastes so good."

"Apple and fruit pie, Sarah bear."

With that, the Earth Keepers stood.

"We have to go now," they said.

"Yes, and so must I," said Angela, "for our work is done."

Sarah stood and hugged all three of the Earth Keepers.

"Thank you so very much for all you have done for me."

The wise man gave the Earth Keepers a small crystal.

"Keep this with you on your return to your lands. It will stop the Takers smelling you and the Clickers seeing you."

The Earth Keepers thanked the wise man.

The Earth Keepers then said their good-byes and left.

"Annie, will you be okay getting home?"

"Yes, child, for I have not far to go."

"I don't understand."

"I am the gatekeeper, I can open a gate to our time anywhere and arrive almost anywhere I wish, so I will be going now, Sarah. May all the luck go with you. It's up to you and Louis from here on in. What's to be done, only you two can do it and bring back peace and calm and normality to the lands of the Mogie. Be brave, child, and have faith in the crystals. They are a very strong source of power. Listen to what the wise person tells you, follow every instruction to the letter, don't take shortcuts no matter how easy it seems, have faith in yourself. Well, child, that's more than plenty from me. I know I have sounded hard to you, but it's the only way that I would have got you to listen to what I have to say without you answering back, like Louis."

Sarah tittered. "You heard everything?"

"Yes, child, I heard all the remarks all the time. I might be getting old, but I am not deaf. Now give me a hug, for I must be on my way."

Sarah hugged Angela and whispered in her ear, "Love you, Annie."

"And I love you too, child. Please be careful and come back home to me safe and in one piece. I will be waiting."

"Yes, Annie, I will, I promise."

"Bye, Annie." There came a small and weak voice from the bed in the corner. "Bye, Louis, protect each other and look after yourself."

"Yes, Annie, I will look after Sarah, I promise."

"Yes, Louis, I know you will. Nana, see you later."

"Say hello to Steven for me."

"I will."

With that, Angela went out the door, closing it softly behind her,

Sarah sat looking across the table at Nana.

"Can I ask you a question, Nana?"

"Of course you can, Sarah bear."

"Well, Nana, I just wanted to know, why me? Why has this all happened to me? All I wanted was a holiday where I could have some fun with the lads."

"Sarah bear, nobody knows what lies in store for us. Our paths are laid out for us. It's our destiny, and we must follow our destiny."

"But, Nana, why me? Nobody asked me what I wanted. It was just dropped on me."

"Sarah bear, you must follow your heart. If you feel your heart is not in it, then you must chose another path. If you want, I can summon Angela to return and bring you home. But one thing I will tell you, I felt like you at the start when I was given this position. I asked, what about my life? Have I to have none? But after I was here for a while, I wanted nothing else but to stay here. Your Aunt Angela felt the same, but both of us grew to love this place, and it pains us to leave. Louis should be as right as rain in a short while. If he is not, then you will have to go on alone. You will have to make up your mind soon, what you want to do.

"What, Nana? Me? Go on on my own? I don't even know what to do or where I am supposed to go or how to do it."

"Okay, Sarah bear, first thing is the thorn has to be replaced. And the second thing is, it must go back to where it came from, and that's under the elder oak, which is inside the black forest. This has to be done sooner than later as the Takers have a new leader called Malful. And he is a mean piece of work. He won't rest till the thorn is destroyed, and you along with it. There is little life left in their own land since they got into the Earth Keepers' lands. Life has been easy for them. They don't have to do any work, they just take what they want. So if they return to their own lands, they will have to work, and that's a dirty word to them. They would rather kill first than return to work. When the thorn is replaced, the spell is activated, then they must return to their own lands, so that's how important it is. Now, Sarah bear, you know as much as I."

"Okay, Nana, now that I know as much as I do, I will stay. But I am doing this for Taz and another slice of your apple and fruit pie."

"Good girl, Sarah bear, I was hoping you would say that, stay I mean, not apple pie."

Sarah laughed. "I know what you meant, Nana."

"Did someone say pie?" There came a little voice from the bed on the far side of the room.

Nana and Sarah both turned to look at where the voice came from, only to see Louis's head appear over the blankets with a grin from ear to ear.

Both Nana and Sarah laughed.

"Did someone say apple and fruit pie?"

"You're supposed to be sick."

"Well, I am better now, Sarah."

"Well, you better get yourself over to the table if you want some pie. You're not getting crumbs all over Nana's bed."

Louis did a double take.

"NANA." He jumped out of the bed and ran to Nana.

"Hello, cupcakes."

Louis put both arms around Nana's neck and hugged her.

"Nana, you won't believe what that witch made us do. Sorry, Nana, I mean Annie."

Nana laughed. "I know."

"But how do you know?"

"Nana is the wise man, I mean wise person. She knows everything that happens in Mogieland," said Sarah.

Louis sat at the table beside Sarah.

"Here, Louis," said Sarah, "here's some pie. That should keep you quiet for a little while."

"Thanks, Nana. All I had to eat for ages was fruit, and you know, Nana, you can get sick of fruit when you have to eat it all day every day, and, Nana, what's them things like big dogs out there with six legs? I think I remember seeing one when the Earth Keepers were bringing me here. And when we got of them mud things."

"They're a cross between a lion and a Great Dane. One of the wise men crossed them years ago, and over time, they have turned out to what they are today."

"Yes, Nana, but did I count six legs?"

"Yes, you did, cupcakes, and they are called the Tallis. Now back to more important things."

"Louis, be quiet for a while. Nana wants to tell us something and just eat your pie."

"He's okay, Sarah bear. You enjoy your pie, cupcakes. Now, Sarah bear, we have to bring you up-to-date on the thorn. It has to go back to where it belongs, and that is in the base of the elder oak inside the black forest.

Now, Sarah bear, you have to know that when you leave here, you will only have protection as far as the edge of my lands. When you cross into the swamp, you will be on your own with no protection."

"No, she won't, Nana, be on her own, that is," Louis said between mouthfuls of pie, "I am going with her."

"Good man, cupcakes, I was hoping you would. On to what I was saying. The Takers are up in arms, they are everywhere. There is the full nation of Takers out there looking for you, Sarah bear, and you, cupcakes. And the thorn, they will do anything within their power to get the thorn from you, so just be careful. They are a very clever lot, them Takers, so you will have to try to stay ahead of them at all times."

Nana got up and crossed the kitchen, picking up a flower pot. She returned to the table; she placed the pot in front of Sarah.

"Reach inside, Sarah bear."

Sarah put her hand into the jar. Taking her hand out of the jar, she held a small crystal in her grip. Or crystals. There were four all joined together, like an X and a whistle.

"This is the only help that I can give to you. You will know when to use it. Keep it safe, for it may save your life. The whistle is for when you are in a position that seems impossible. It will bring you help. Now that's all I can do for you. Jack is at the door, he will bring you across my lands to the swamp's edge. I want you both to put this on."

Nana opened a bowl of funny-looking cream; it was a green color. Louis lifted the cream to his nose and smelled it.

"There's no smell."

"You need to put this on, and there's no smell. It will kill the odors from your bodies so the Takers can't smell you."

"Okay, Nana, and thanks for the crystal." Sarah stood up and went around to Nana and gave her a hug.

"Thank you, Nana."

Louis did the same.

The two kids started to put the cream on.

"What's this for, Nana?"

"Louis, are you with it at all? It is to stop the Takers getting your scent. They have poor eyesight, but they can smell you miles away. This cream stops them getting your scent."

After they had put on the cream, it vanished into their skins.

Nana got up and walked to the back door with the kids.

"Sorry everything seems to be rushed, but the quicker you get the thorn replaced, the quicker we can all relax."

Opening the back door, Nana told the kids she was going to miss them and to hurry back but to watch each other and be careful.

"We will," they both said.

Outside the back door, Jack was standing, waiting.

The kids went over to Jack and rubbed his head and hugged him.

"Can Jack not come with us, Nana?"

"I am sorry, Louis, but if Jack leaves my lands, then he will lose all his powers, and he would die in seconds. And I don't think we would want that to happen to him, would we?"

"No, Nana, we would not."

They all started to head off toward the swamp.

Louis turned and said good-bye to Nana.

"I will look after Sarah, Nana, and I will make sure she is safe."

Nana said bye to Sarah and Louis, and she nodded to Louis.

"I know you will, cupcakes, I know you will."

Nana stood at the door waving and watching till Jack and the kids disappeared into the trees. One single tear ran down Nana's face as she whispered, "Please be safe and come back to me soon." She was sad that she could not give the kids more help or even go with them, but there was only so much she could do; the rest depended on them.

Nana went back into the house and sat at the kitchen table. There was nothing she could do now but wait for the kids to return. This was going to be the hardest part, waiting.

Angela and Steven

Steven was fast asleep in the campsite dreaming of battles, castles, and kings. He was in such a deep sleep he never heard the noise or saw the flash of light, which lit up the whole area.

Angela stepped out of the light, looking around.

"I think this is where I am supposed to be."

But she could not see Steven.

"That's odd. I am never wrong."

Staying quite for a few seconds, she could hear Steven snoring. The sound was coming from the other side of the bramble row.

Angela took a crystal from inside a bag around her waist. Holding the crystal out in front of her, it shone through the hedge. Angela could now see through the hedge, like looking through a window. She could see Steven rolled up in a ball fast asleep. Angela called out his name; Steven did not stir. Angela called a second time, only a little louder. Still Steven did not move. Angela shouted the third time. She saw Steven moving. Angela held the crystal out with the full length of her arms; a hole appeared in the hedge.

Steven heard his name being called. He thought he was dreaming, then he heard his name being called a second time. He started to sit up, rubbing his eyes when all of a sudden, a large hole appeared in the hedge right in front of him. Steven started to rub his eyes again.

"No way," he said out loud. He could see Angela standing on the other side of the hole, holding out something that was shining.

"No way," he said again. "She is a witch."

Steven called out, "Annie?"

"Yes, Steven."

"Annie, is that you?"

"Yes, child."

"Did you do that to the hedge?"

"Yes, child, why did you not answer me when I called you?"

"I was asleep."

"Well, you're awake now, child. Come on, get up, and come with me."

"Come with you where?"

"We have things to do."

"Where's Louis? He went to find you."

"He okay, he's doing a message for me. Now come on, and we have things to do, and the sooner, the better."

"How did you do that with the hedge?"

"I will explain all that to you later, but we must go now."

"Okay, but where are we going?" Steven asked as he stepped through the hole in the hedge.

"Well, first we must go to the house to collect something."

"Where?"

"I will explain on the way to the house."

While they walked to Nana's house, Angela explained to Steven everything that had happened up to now as much as she could.

Steven was left with his mouth open.

When they arrived at the house, Angela told Steven to wait in the house for her and to take the three bags of salt from the larder. Angela went around the back of the house to the garden shed. Taking the key from over the door, she opened the shed door. She scanned the inside of the shed.

"Ah, yes, there it is." An old wooden box sat on the shelf on its own. Angela crossed the shed and picked up the box, carefully opening the lid. The crystal inside was shining.

"Good."

Angela took the crystal from the box and placed it into a bag around her waist. She closed the lid and replaced the box back on the shelf, and she left the shed. She headed across to the house. When she got near the house, she called Steven.

Steven was standing at the window, watching Angela coming across the back toward the house. When she called him, Steven ran out the door.

"Yes, Annie."

"Okay, child, it's time. We must go." Annie sat on the ground and told Steven to sit beside her.

When Steven was sitting down, Angela placed two crystals in front of them, one on top of the other. The bottom crystal started to shine, and the light went up through the second crystal into the sky.

Steven looked. "What's happening, Annie?"

"Wait and see, child."

The crystal got brighter; the one on top started to spin. As it spun, a hole started to open in front of them.

Steven held on to Annie.

The hole got bigger and spreaded out wider till Steven and Annie were inside. There were colors everywhere; it felt nice and warm.

Steven could see everything: Nana's house, the Glen of the Downs, Wicklow Bay, even the Dublin Mountains. "This is cool, Annie."

Annie leaned forward and moved the bottom crystal to the right. As she did, things started to change.

Steven could now see different things: a black forest, a mucky swamp, another black forest with a few green trees in patches.

"Where's that, Annie?"

"It's Mogieland. That's where we are going."

Steven could now see a colorful area in the middle of the swamp and a house in the middle of the colored area.

"Is that where we are going?"

"No, to the right just at the edge of the black forest and the swamp."

The top crystal slowed down.

Then they were sitting just inside the tree line in the black forest.

Angela took two small crystals and handed them to Steven.

"If you are the right person, you will know how to use these and when to use them." She placed them into Steven's hand.

Steven took the crystals and put them both into his pocket.

"Now, I will tell you what you must do before you go from here."

"And you must pay full attention."

"Yes, Annie, I will."

But before Annie could say a word, the noise from the distance started to get louder and louder.

"What's that, Annie?"

"Quiet, Steven, please."

Steven looked at Annie. "Why?"

Annie put her fingers to her lips.

She whispered to Steven, "Move more into the trees."

The noise was very loud.

Click, click, click, click, and *click.*

Steven and Annie both looked up together.

They could see a few large insects flying by then more and more till the sky was black with them.

"What are they, Annie?"

"They are the Clickers. They must have been summoned to flight."

"Why, Annie?"

"I really don't know. They never swarm all together unless they are summoned."

"Then who summoned them?"

"I don't know the answer to that either, but I think the only one with the power to summon them is the wise man."

Steven and Annie stooped down behind a large tree.

They waited for a while, and then they saw the Clickers flying back from the way they had come. Each Clicker had a Taker in their claws.

"What are they carrying, Annie?"

"It looks like Takers."

"Takers, Annie? It looks like they are taken."

"Yes, Steven, and they won't be missed."

"Yes, but there's hundreds of them, maybe thousands."

"Yes, Steven, there is. And the more, the better. Well, I suppose I should not blame the branches for a bad trunk."

"You what and what, Annie?"

"You can't blame the Takers for their leader's actions."

"Oh, well, I understand that."

Annie looked at Steven. "Well, good."

"Are they like bees, Annie?"

"I suppose their behavior is somewhat the same. But they are a lot bigger, and a lot nastier. But only when they are provoked. Other than that, they are quite harmless."

"Well, Annie, I am no expert on bees, but don't they swarm? For no reason, they had to be provoked."

"You know what, Steven? You just might be right."

Takers

The word had spread across all the lands that there was a new leader among the Takers. Other than the Takers keeping guard over the Earth Keepers, all other Takers were to return to the swamp at the safe path to the wise man's lands.

Nobody would disobey the instructions from a new leader. Well, not till they got to know him.

Malful stood on the hill overlooking the swamp. He looked across the Takers that had gathered. There must be twenty-five thousand. He had to put a plan in place; he knew that the gap into the wise man's lands was too narrow to let more than six or eight Takers through at a time, and the Tallis on the other side would wipe out the whole twenty-five thousand bit by bit. Malful called thirty of the Takers and instructed them to take ten Takers each and surround the wise man's lands and look for another way into the lands and to let him know as soon as they found another way in to send word to him as fast as possible. They were not to go in, but they were to wait for instructions from him.

Malful thought to himself, *There has to be more than one way in and out of the wise man's lands. Otherwise, how did the strangers get in and out?* Malful sat and watched as the Takers started to become uneasy. He could see the Tallis across the field; they were just sitting and watching the Takers. Most of them, if not all, had seen Malgit's sudden and swift death, and as long as they were there, his Takers would not enter, for it meant certain death to anyone who crossed into the wise man's lands.

He was now hoping that one of the groups he sent out would come back soon with good news. Otherwise, the Takers would lose interest in the plan at hand and would start to drift away. All he could do for now was wait. While he was waiting, he watched the Tallis. Two of the Tallis got up and left. A short time later, the Tallis returned. One of the Tallis was carrying something in his mouth. He swung his head from left to right very fast and let go of what was in his mouth. The thing that was in his mouth went flying through the air in the direction of Malful. It landed about ten feet from where he was standing. When it stopped rolling, it stopped at Malful's feet. Malful looked at the item: it was a head of a Taker.

This was a warning, and Malful knew this. But where did they get the head? Unless one of the groups he sent out crossed into the wise man's lands. *Fools, they were supposed to report back to me.*

Malful could smell something up wind; this he did not need now. It was the smell of the Clickers. If they came this way, his Takers were out in the open and were easy pickings for the Clickers. Then he heard the noise. It was very loud, too loud for a swarm of Clickers.

Malful's eyesight was not the best, but even he could see the sky getting dark. It was not a swarm of Clickers, they were swarms and swarms of Clickers.

"This is not good, no, this is not good at all," said Malful. He had about twenty-five thousand Takers there with him. About half of them were out in the open, looking at the skies. He guessed there were twice as many Clickers in the air. There could be as many as twenty thousand Clickers at a guess. If they decided to swoop down on the Takers, it would wipe out over half of the Takers. Malful could do nothing but watch. All the Takers had stopped where they were and were looking up toward the sky at the Clickers. They did not run; they just froze with fear as they watched the Clickers. The Clickers seemed to be flying past the Takers; not one Clicker swooped down. They just flew on in their hundreds as if they were migrating. The leading pack of the Clickers started to turn in a very wide circle. The Takers on the ground stood and watched. The Clickers formed a full circle in the sky, blocking out most of the sky. Some of the Takers that were in the trees came out to watch what was going on; they had never seen so many Clickers in flight.

This was all new to them.

Malful was still standing, watching. He guessed that all the swarms of Clickers were in flight. He wondered what could have caused this. Malful looked around at his Takers again. They were still standing, watching the Clickers. Malful took the time, unnoticed by anybody. He back slowly into the trees. None of the Takers noticed Malful backing to the trees. Just as Malful got to safe ground, the Clickers swooped. They swooped in hundreds at a time, straight down on top of the shocked Takers. Before the Takers had time to turn, their numbers were halved. Not very many made it to the safety of the trees. Over five thousand were carried away in the first swoop. As the first row of Clickers flew back to the sky with a Taker, the second row started in, and this was repeated over and over again till there were no more Takers left in the open. When the Clickers flew back to their own lands, there were fifteen thousand to eighteen thousand less Takers. Malful watched all this from the safety of the trees. This was not a good thing for him, he would, or he should say. Malgit would have not lost as many Takers if he went through the lands of the Clickers. He had expected to lose some of the Takers up here, trying to capture the strangers, but he never thought it would be this many. Malful waited till there were no Clickers left in the sky to break his cover. He screamed orders to all the remaining Takers to gather around him. He waited till this was done, and then he stood out in the open and addressed them.

"This is what happens when we have strangers in our lands, and they join forces with the Clickers and the Vox. Who's to blame? Well, I will tell you. It's the Earth Keepers because they have hid these strangers in their caves, and they have aided them in their journey to the wise man, and they are the cause of this slaughter here today. Now maybe you will understand why it is so important that we use every means possible to catch and kill these strangers. So I ask you here, who will follow me and not rest till we catch these strangers in our lands so that we can avenge the deaths of our fellow Takers?"

Malful looked down on the Takers; they seemed to be undecided.

"I ask you again, are you going to let your friends' and families' deaths here today be for nothing? Are you prepared to follow me to rid Mogieland of these strangers?"

A few Takers in the middle of the crowd started to chant, "Kill the strangers." More and more joined in. "Kill the strangers." Malful knew he had the Takers where he wanted them.

"Well, what are we waiting for? Surround the wise man's lands, find another way in, search every inch till you find a way in. Now go, avenge you family and friends, kill the strangers, rid our lands of these troublemakers."

The Takers started moving in all directions. Malful grinned.

"They will not take from me what is mine. And all these lands are mine. I will be the most powerful leader ever. And nobody will ever challenge my leadership. Not now, not ever."

He did not care for losses. All that concerned Malful was power. He wanted to be more powerful than Malgit and to hold that power as long as he did. That was his final plan, and if every Taker perished in the execution of it, so be it.

He watched as the Takers spreaded out in every direction possible.

"That's it, fools, go find the strangers," he said out loud as there was no one around or near to hear him, or so he thought.

But he was not as clever as he was tough.

He did not see the Takers behind the tree at his back.

They sat behind the tree; they dared not moved with fear, for if Malful heard or saw them, it meant certain death. And with what they have just heard, they wanted the chance to tell every Taker in the land just how good a leader Malful was. Malful moved off from where he was to higher ground, still staying in the trees for safety. He was making sure he was well out of the reach of the Clickers if they returned.

And he was sure whoever summoned them would do so again. But not if he stopped them first, and that's something he would enjoy doing.

The Strangest Thing

Sarah and Louis entered the trees. As they did, Jack let out a little moan. "What's wrong, Jack?"

He cocked his head into the air and let out a long howl.

He rubbed his nose on the back of Sarah's hand.

"Oh, what's up, baby?"

Jack started to walk backward.

"Oh, I think I understand. You have to stop here, you can't go any farther. Well, that's okay, Jack. Thank you for getting us this far."

Sarah put her arms around Jack's neck and gave him a big hug. Louis hugged Jack as well.

"I am going to miss you, Jack."

"And so am I," said Louis.

Jack backed away and sat on the ground.

"Why is he not coming, Sarah?"

"I think that's as far as he can go, but he will wait there for a while."

"Oh, I think I understand."

"Okay, Louis, I suppose it's up to us now."

"Yep, I suppose it is. Shall we?"

"Yes, we shall."

As they were leaving, they could hear the howl of the other Tallis.

Jack stood on all six legs; he howled again and took off.

"That's funny." said Sarah, "There must be something wrong."

"Why do you think that?"

"The way Jack is acting."

"I suppose we will find out sooner or later."

"Yes, we will, Louis. Yes, we will."

The two started off again, making their way through the trees.

They came to an area where all the trees had died and fallen. The area was as big as football grounds.

"I wonder what happened here."

"I don't know," said Sarah, "but it's odd that all the trees should die and fall in one area and nowhere else."

"Yes, I suppose." They started to cross the area, climbing over stumps and fallen trees.

The whistle Nana gave Sarah fell from her pocket.

Louis noticed this and picked up the whistle.

Looking at it, he wondered if it was like the Earth Keepers'. Was there any sound going to come out of this one? *Ah, well I will never find out unless I try it.*

Louis put the whistle to his lips and blew.

As he did, Sarah turned and saw him.

"Louis, what are you doing?"

"Trying out this whistle. It's a good thing I did because it's broken. There's no sound from it."

"Give me that. You know what Nana said. Only use it when we are in trouble. You're some help."

Louis looked at Sarah.

"But nothing happened."

"But we don't know that. Come on, and please don't do anything till I ask you please."

"Oh, okay, but I don't see what I have done wrong."

As soon as Louis said wrong, the noise started to come from the distance.
Sarah looked at Louis. "What's that?"

"I don't know."

The noise got louder and louder.

"I know that sound, it's the Clickers."

"The what?"

"The Clickers. Stay in the trees."

The noise was now becoming deafening, and the sky started to darken.
Both Louis and Sarah looked up.

"Oh shit, where did they all come from?"

"I think you called them, Louis, when you blew on that whistle."

"Me? I did that? No way, Sarah, I can't even get a dog to come to me
when I whistle."

"It doesn't matter. Get down, get under the falling trees."

She did not have to tell him twice. They both got under the trees together.
The both of them watched the sky get darker and darker as swarm after
swarm of Clickers passed overhead.

Louis tapped Sarah on the shoulder and pointed across the clearing at
five Clickers, who had landed. They were sniffing the ground.

"I hope the cream Nana gave us works."

"Shusssssssssssss."

They watched as two of the Clickers started to head over in their
direction, sniffing the ground as they went.

Other than the low *click click*, Sarah could hear Louis breathing; the
Clickers were only feet away from where they hid.

Sarah looked at the crystals Nana had given her, but there was nothing
coming from them.

The sweat started to run down her forehead onto her nose; she was not even
able to move, not even to wipe the sweat away. One of the Clickers was almost
on top of them. She looked over at Louis. He had his eyes shut tight.

The Clicker was so close now that Sarah could see the long beelike eye of the Clicker. She was watching him so close that she never saw the Clicker farthest away burst into flames. The Clicker that was standing inches away clicked loud twice and took flight. The noise of the Clicker taking flight frightened Sarah so much that she screamed.

The other three Clickers took flight after the first one.

Sarah looked at Louis; she could see tears running down his face.

"You can open your eyes now, they're gone. Are you crying?"

"Me? No," he said as he wiped the tears away, "I am sweating, it's so warm here."

They both got up from where they were.

"I wonder what happened to that Clicker?" said Louis, pointing to the pile of ashes on the ground.

"I think I know. It was the Vox."

"But funny there is no sign of them, and yet they're the only ones that could do that."

"I am not even going to say I understand what you're on about because I don't, and I don't want to understand. This place is weird."

Sarah just shook her head. "Boys, I will never understand them."

"Let's wait here for a while till things calm down a little."

"Yeah, I think that was a little too close for comfort."

They both sat where they were, watching for movement.

After a while, they both emerged from their hiding place. They went over to the pile of ashes that was a Clicker earlier.

"There's no fresh soil anywhere around here."

"No what, Sarah?"

"Fresh soil. When the Vox come out of the ground, they leave a small hole and clay around the edges, but there's none here."

Louis scratched his head.

"I don't know what you're talking about."

"How did the Clicker burst into flames? It had to be the Vox."

"Okay, I understand that."

"But there's no trace of the Vox. Maybe it was the crystal."

"No, they were in my pocket. It had to be the Vox."

"Okay, Vox or no Vox, can we go? I don't like this place, this place is like waking up from a nightmare only to find you were awake all the time, and I would like very much to get out of here."

"Which way are we going?"

"I don't know." Sarah took a crystal from her pocket. She faced south, nothing. She faced west, nothing. She then faced east and still nothing. When she faced north, the crystal started to glow.

"Right, Louis, it's this way. Let's go."

They started to climb over tree trunks and branches.

Louis roared, "I HATE THIS KIP!"

"What's wrong with you now? And keep your voice down."

"That's what's wrong." Louis was pointing at his leg.

Sarah looked down at Louis's leg. There was a cut about three inches long on his leg just under his knee.

"Wait, sit down and let me have a look."

Louis sat on a tree stump. "I hate this dump."

"Quiet and let me see." The cut was bleeding too fast for Sarah's liking. Her face went pale.

"What's wrong? It's only a cut."

"I know, but I don't like blood, and there's a lot of blood here."

"Ah, leave it. It will be grand."

Sarah wasn't sure. Louis's sock was full of blood.

"Wait, I remember something I saw."

Sarah took out some crystals from her bag. One by one, she placed them over Louis's cut leg. When she placed the fourth crystal over the cut, it started to glow. She moved it in an anticlockwise movement over the cut. The wound started to close.

"You're spending too much time with that witch, I mean, Annie."

"Louis, would you, for once in your life, just shut up?" Sarah put the crystal back into her bag.

"There, that should keep you in one piece for a while."

Louis looked back down at his leg. The cut was gone.

"Hay, Sarah, I suppose I better keep my mouth shut from now on, or you will put a spell on me."

"Well, maybe I will, but thanks would have been nice."

"You're welcome."

"I give up on you. I am now beginning to understand what Annie means when she says there's no hope for you."

"Ah, come on, Sarah, I was only joking."

"Yes, whatever. Now can we get on with what we were doing?"

"Ah, come on, Sarah, I am sorry and thanks."

"Are you coming, or are you staying there?" Sarah continued to climb over the fallen trees.

"Yes, I am coming, mini witch," Louis muttered.

All Together Again

"Okay, Steven, you're now on your own. You know what to do."

"Yes, Annie, can you not come with me?"

"No, Steven, I must go back. You have the crystals and the salt."

"Yes, Annie."

"Okay"—Annie hugged Steven—"be safe."

"I will, Annie, and thanks."

Annie rubbed a crystal. It started to glow. After a few seconds, the gateway opened. Annie stepped into the glow, and as quickly as it opened, it closed.

Steven was now standing by himself.

Steven started off toward the north, trying to remember everything that Annie had told him.

After a while, Steven was going through some woods when he froze.

He could see shapes and movement ahead of him.

Steven got behind a large tree and watched. The shapes were coming toward him; there were two of them.

Steven ducked down as far as he could and waited.

The shapes got closer; he could hear voices now.

"Is that Louis? No, it can't be."

"How far more do you think we have to go, Sarah?"

"I don't know."

"Well, I am getting tired."

"Yes, Louis, and so am I. Tell you what, when we get over there to that big tree, we will rest up for a while."

"Okay, that's sounds good. I wish I had something to eat."

"So do I."

As they approached the tree, something jumped out at them.

"MOMMY!" Louis roared. Sarah started crying.

"Ha-ha, it's okay, it's only me," said Steven.

"I am going to kill you!" Louis roared. Sarah ran toward Steven and wrapped her arms around his neck, hugging him and crying at the same time.

"Oh, it's good to see you. How did you get here?"

Louis had calmed down. "Yeah, how did you get here?"

"Annie brought me here to help you."

"Good old Annie. Bet you she brought you through that gateway of hers, and you say she's not a witch."

Steven did not answer Louis.

"We are going to rest here for a while."

"That's grand, Sarah, but not for long. We have to keep moving."

"That's okay, but we need to have a rest just for a short while, then we will be ready to go."

"Hay, Louis, these are for you." Steven handed Louis a Bounty bar and a Mars bar, and he also gave the same to Sarah.

"I love you, Steve. I thought you would have eaten them all."

"No, Louis, I kept your share for you."

Louis sat down and started into the Mars bar. Sarah put hers into her bag.

Sarah sat down with Steven.

"How much did Annie tell you?"

"Almost everything up to now, except the part where you went missing. What happened to you?"

"That's for another day, but you know then what we have to do."

"Yes, I do. Replace the thorn and put it back to where it belongs."

"Yes, Steven, but by the looks of things, it won't be too easy to do. You have no idea of the things that's going on in this place. It's a nightmare."

"I know it won't be easy, and Annie told me most of the things that's going on here. But together, we can do it."

Louis had finished eating the Mars bar and the Bounty bar.

"Well, that was much needed."

"Well, seems you're fed. Are you ready to go?"

"I suppose."

"Are you ready, Sarah?"

"Yes, Steven, I am as ready as I am ever going to be."

"Okay, so we still have some distance to travel, so let's go."

Steven led the way followed by Sarah and then Louis.

"We are keeping you where we can see you so we don't lose you again."

"No hope of that, I am sticking to you both like glue."

"Well, make sure you do. I don't want to be the one to tell Annie that we have lost you again, Now that would be a nightmare."

"Yes, and I am not going to be the one to tell Annie the next time."

Missing Takers

Malful had sent groups of Takers in every direction to look for the strangers and to kill them. Two of these groups were travelling along the northeast border lines of the wise man's lands and, after much discussion along the way, decided to join forces, doubling their strength. One of the Takers took leadership. This young Taker was named Balgus. He was the leader of the biggest group. The leader of the smaller group became his right-hand man. His name was Tricore. As they travelled along the border of the wise man's lands, they were joined by loose Takers returning to the main body. Balgus had started out from the main camp where the Clickers had taken two-thirds of the Takers. With only thirty Takers starting off, now he had nearly eight hundred followers. They had searched and searched for a way into the wise man's lands but could not find a way. Balgus decided to camp for a while to give the Takers a rest. Balgus was sitting at the base of a tree when Tricore came up to him with three Takers.

"Is there something wrong, Tricore?"

"Yes, Balgus, I think so. You have to hear what these Takers have to say."

"Okay, sit, all of you, and tell me."

The three Takers and Tricore sat facing Balgus.

One of the Takers explained to Balgus that after the Clicker attack, he and his two friends were hiding behind a tree trunk when Malful came to where they were hiding. He did not see them, and he stood there alone.

Then he told the story of how Malful was willing to lose all the Takers to gain full control and power. And he was prepared to do this any way possible, even if it meant the loss of all the Takers in the Mogieland. When the Takers were sent to find a way into the wise man's lands, Malful stood and called them fools.

"That is all we have to tell you, Balgus."

"I want to thank you for brining this news to me. Now go and rest, and you have no more to fear from Malful as long as you are within this group. Now go and get some rest."

When the three Takers went and rejoined the main group, Balgus and Tricore sat together.

"What are going to do about this, Balgus? We have to do something."

"We are going to build our numbers till we are ready to challenge Malful, and I want you to take control."

"Me? Take control? You can't mean leader."

"Yes, I do, and it will not be easy to challenge Malful. We will have to be one step ahead of him at all times."

"That won't be hard to do."

"It will not be so easy, Tricore, as Malful has a lot of hard-line followers that are with him from the very start, and they are more powerful than we are. Let us take our time and build our numbers first. We also have them three Takers out there telling anyone that will listen the story of Malful after the Clicker raid and what he is prepared to do to gain power."

"Do you think the Takers will be happy about this?"

"We could add on a little more, like we were sold out to the Clickers for safe passage for Malful and some of his followers through the Clickers' lands."

"So what do we do now?"

We keep looking for a way into the wise man's lands as we were told to do by our leader, and we will increase our numbers along the way.

Now, my friend, rest up, and we will start off again in our search soon.

Tricore got up and returned to the main body of Takers. He passed groups of Takers along the way, and they were all talking about Malful.

He stopped at one of the groups and planted the extra bit of news about the safe passage through the Clickers' lands for Malful and a few of his followers, and the price they had paid for this. This started off more talk, which would spread fast among the Takers.

Tricore carried on to a spot at the base of a tree. He placed his hands on the tree and started to drain some life from the tree. As he did so, he watched the Takers go from group to group, telling their news.

This could be the best thing that could happen for Malful, or it could mean his total downfall. *I hope it's the latter.* Tricore sat down at the base of the tree. He was taking a rest, for he was unsure of when he would get a chance to do so again. That was if he was to live long enough to get the time to rest again.

The Trio

Steven, Sarah, and Louis had crossed over the open ground of fallen trees and were now safe in the black forest. Well, as safe as possible.

They still had a long way to go. The black forest was harder to get through; the trees and brambles were like a wall. They had only travelled about ten feet, and it had taken them a long time.

"There has to be an easier way to get through this."

"I don't know, Steven, it seems to be the same everywhere."

"Can you not use your crystals, Sarah?"

"I don't know, Louis, but I suppose anything is worth a try. Otherwise, we are going to be here forever."

Sarah reached into her bag and took out a small-sized crystal. She held it out but nothing. She took a second crystal from her bag and held it out, nothing. She held out the crystal that was around her neck, nothing.

"Well, I guess that answers your question."

They all looked at each other.

"Well, I suppose it's the hard way."

"Looks like that, Steven."

"Hold on, Sarah." Steven reached inside the bag he was carrying. After a few seconds, he pulled out three crystals.

"Where did you get them, Steven?" asked Louis.

"From Annie before she left."

"Left? You mean she was here?"

"Yes, she dropped me off at the clearing."

"And she never came over here to say hello."

"She's not able to leave the gateway, except to enter her own land or the wise man's."

"Now are you happy with that, Louis? Maybe we can get on with what we are doing."

"Yes, Sarah." Steven held out the first crystal, nothing. He then held out the second crystal, nothing. "The last one," he said, holding out the third crystal. Nothing.

"No wait."

"Wait for what, Sarah?"

"Just wait a second."

Sarah took a crystal back out of her bag and stood beside Steven, holding the crystal out at arm's length alongside Steven's crystal. The two crystals started to glow.

"Look," said Louis, "they're glowing."

Sarah smiled at Steven.

The bramble started to withdraw, and a pathway started to appear through the bramble.

"Look, called Louis, "it's clearing, we will be able to get through without getting caught in every thorn. And hay, did you two take lessons from the witch?"

"Ah, Louis, will you ever pack in the witch thing? It's not funny anymore."

"It was only a joke, Sarah."

"Come on, you two, it's time to go now that the way is clear."

Steven put the crystal back in his bag, and Sarah put her crystal back into her bag.

And they started off again for the elder oak.

Walking was much easier now.

After a few minutes, Louis said, "Hay, are you watching this?"

"What?"

"The brambles are closing behind us."

Sarah and Steven both looked back only to see what Louis was saying was right. The brambles were closing behind them as they passed through.

"That's odd."

"Everything is odd in this place, Sarah."

"Yes, you don't have to tell me, Steven."

"How are we going to get back?"

"The same way we came, Louis, and we will use witchcraft."

"Ha-ha, who's funny now?"

Sarah looked a Louis. "It was supposed to be smart, not funny."

"Okay, you two, we will worry about getting back when we get to the elder oak and do whatever it is we are supposed to do. So for now, can we stop fighting and be smart among ourselves and worry about what's out there ahead of us?"

"Okay," said Louis.

"Okay," said Sarah.

"Anyway, Sarah, I meant to ask you, where's this fifth thorn?"

Sarah pointed at her hair.

"In my hair. It's the hairpin that I have had for years. It's the missing thorn, so Tazmaz tells me."

Louis butted in, "Who's Tazmaz, Sarah?"

"He is the leader of the Earth Keepers. He is the one who told me all about what happened here and how the fifth thorn went missing after a visit to his lands by Stephanie."

"Stephanie? No way."

Steven and Louis both just looked at Sarah. She took the thorn from her hair and held it out for the lads to see. Then she replaced it back into her hair.

"I don't know, and nobody else does either. It went missing the same time she left Mogieland."

"But—"

"No more questions, Louis, because I don't know the answers."

Steven took the hint as well.

"Okay, but Stephanie has a lot to answer for when we get home."

"Yes, she has, Steven," said Sarah.

"I wonder how far we have to go now," said Louis.

"I don't think it is too far."

"Okay, Sarah, I will take your word for it."

"Well, Grandma said the elder oak was just inside the black forest, and the crystals are telling us to go this way, so I think we are almost there or very close."

They started off on their journey again. It was slow as the black forest growth was very thick again. None of them spoke, and none of them noticed they were being watched, for not too far away were two Takers. They had seen the strangers approaching. They stayed very quiet and watched. They knew they would pass where they were, and then they would strike.

Steven had taken the lead, followed by Sarah and then by Louis. They were too busy trying to get through the growth to notice anything.

When they did notice something was wrong, it was too late; the two Takers came out of hiding two feet away from Steven.

"Well, well, what have we here? Looks like we have a few trespassers on our land, and the penalty for trespassing is death," said the bigger Taker of the two.

Sarah and Louis both got close behind Steven.

"And where do you think you are off to?"

"We're out for a stroll," said Steven.

"A stroll, is it? Well, you're on my land, and you have to pay."

"Pay what?"

"A fee for using our land and the damage you have done."

"What damage are you talking about? I mean after what you have done to this land, you can't be serious. Okay, so what's the fee?"

"Well, we require a small token."

"Token like what?"

"Well, let's say for your safe passage, something small. Let's say a thorn."

"What's a thorn?"

"Don't act silly with me. You know what I am talking about."

Steven turned and looked at Sarah.

"Well, if it's the thorn they want, then I think it's only fair that we should give them the thorn, what do you think, Sarah?"

"No way, Steven, not after all we have went through."

"Well, if we don't give it to them, they will kill us and take it. But if we give them the thorn, then they will let us go."

Steven turned to the Taker. "Is that right?"

"You give me the thorn, and then we will see."

"One way or another, I don't think we are going to win, are we?"

The Taker just kept looking at Steven.

Steven shook his head. "Well, I suppose I have to trust you, Steven."

He turned around to face Sarah. "We will have to give them the thorn."

"No, Steven, if you do that, then everything is lost."

"I don't think we have a choice, everything is lost now. These two Takers could kill us here and now and just take the thorn."

Steven turned back to the Taker.

"Okay, you win. But you have to promise that you will let us go, and I give you the thorn."

"Give me the thorn first, and then I will make up my mind."

Steven reached inside his bag.

What happened next was like a flash. The kids were left with their mouths open.

Both the Takers fell to the ground, headless.

Steven composed himself.

Sarah screamed, putting her hands up to her face, "What happened?"

"I don't know. Something flashed, passed us, and they just fell."

"I know," said Louis.

Both Steven and Sarah looked at Louis. "What?"

"It was Jack."

"Don't be silly, Louis, the Tallis are not allowed outside the wise man's lands as well as that, they have no powers out here."

"It was Jack, I saw him."

"Well then, how come we did not see him?"

"I don't know, but it was Jack. I know it was."

There was a noise in the bushes just in front of them.

The kids froze.

Steven could hear Sarah crying behind him.

Steven still had his hand it the bag. His hand tightened around the bag of salt he was holding. They all watched as the bushes started to part.

Louis roared, "Hello, Grandad!"

Sarah and Steven could not believe their eyes.

"Grandad."

All three ran to their Grandad.

"Slow down, slow down, you will knock me over."

"Grandad, what are you doing out here?"

"Ah, some crows robbed a bag of seed, and I followed them here."

"I believe that, Grandad."

"It's true, Louis." Grandad winked at him.

"Okay, so where are we at?"

"We are to put this thorn back in the elder oak."

"And are you close, Steven?"

"We don't know, Grandad."

"Well, I best let you get on with it, and I will see you later back at the house."

"Are you not going to help us?"

"I can't, Sarah, it's forbidden. For you to get any help, you must complete this task on your own."

"Can you not even stay a while?"

"I have to find the bag of seed, Sarah."

"Okay, Grandad, see you later. Can you tell us we are even close?"

"I don't know, Steven, I am not sure of this area. It's all strange to me. See you later, kids, and be careful." Grandad went back into the bushes and was gone.

The kids looked at each other with puzzled expressions.

Louis smiled and whispered, "See ya, Jack."

"Grandad was in a bit of a hurry. You would think he would have stayed and gave us a hand."

"I think he already did."

"He what, Louis?"

"Oh, nothing, Steven." Louis smiled.

"Right," said Steven, "that was a close call. We have to make sure we don't get caught like that again."

"We are on our own, I don't know what happened there. But we were lucky to get away with that. We can't count on luck all the time."

"I don't know how far it is to the elder oak, but I think we should keep going till we get there. We don't know how many more of them things are around, so no more rest breaks or anything. I just want to get this thorn back to where it belongs and get out of this place back to where we belong."

"I think we have more help than you think, Steven."

"I don't know, Louis, but we can't rely on anyone or anything. We have to do this, and we have to do it as fast as we can. And get the hell out of here. This place gives me the creeps, I don't like it."

"No, and I don't like this place either. I only like Grandma's apple and fruit pie. It's the only thing that's nice in this place, and that's the place where I want to be."

"Oh yeah, Louis, food. We could have been killed there, and you can only think of pie."

"That's not true, Steven, I am hungry."

Sarah reached into her bag and took out a Mars bar.

"Here, Louis, maybe this will keep you quiet for a while."

"Thanks, Sarah."

As soon as Louis said hungry, Steven realized just how hungry he was. It's a while since he had eaten.

Sarah then took the Bounty bar from her bag and gave it to Steven.

"Thanks, Sarah, but what about you?"

"Don't worry about me, I have been eating fruit."

Sarah was feeling a little hungry as well, but she was logical.

"Well, when we get the thorn replaced, we can eat all we want but not till then, so let's get this over with."

Louis and Steven both agreed.

"Well, seems we're all agreed. Let's get going. And finish what we started out to do."

Finishing off the Mars bar, Louis said, "I am with you on that."

"Thanks, Louis, and what about you, Steven? Are you ready?"

"Guess I am."

"Come on then, let's move. And, boys, please don't throw the wrappers on the ground. The Takers will be able to tell where we are from the smell of the wrapper."

"Are you for real, Sarah?"

"Yes, Steven, the Takers have a very good sense of smell. They can smell things miles away."

Both the lads put the wrappers into their pockets.

The Battle

Tricore had started his group moving again. Watching the group pass by him, he was sure that group was much bigger than when they stopped for a rest. Yes, there must be at least twice the amount of Takers than before the rest period. They had travelled about halfway around the wise man's lands and still no sign of a way into the wise man's lands. And they could see the Tallis following and watching them. Even if they found a way in to the wise man's lands, he did not think they wanted to face the Tallis, and he was sure the rest of the Takers would refuse to go in, even under the threat of death. No, if he did find a way in to the wise man's lands, he would leave that for Malful to enter or some of his followers. His instructions were to find a way into the wise man's lands, nothing more, and report back to Malful, and that's what he would do.

The Takers had stopped up front, and by the time Tricore noticed, they had all stopped. Tricore made his way to the front of the line.

"What's wrong up here?"

To the left were the bodies of two Takers. Both were headless.

Tricore knew this was the work of the Tallis.

But that can't be. This was outside the wise man's area, unless the Tallis had gotten new powers that the Takers did not know about. If this was so, then they were all in big trouble right here and now. Tricore felt very uneasy. He ordered his group to stay with the main body and to move and move fast. This was not a place he wanted to in for long, but the issue still remains. How did the Tallis get out of the wise man's area? He would find out later. It was too dangerous to stay around now. He had to move all the Takers before any unrest started. With what the Clickers did to the Takers, he did not feel his people were up to an encounter with the Tallis. Not just yet. Tricore kept the Takers moving till they came to the stream, which was a safe distance from the bodies of the Takers, and his people were at ease. There was talk from some of the Takers that they wanted to go back to their own lands, while there were some that would go back there. But they knew they would not be allowed, and they knew that Malful would not rest till the strangers were dead and he had full control of the Mogieland. They felt they were in a nowhere place, and Tricore knew this. Now he made a promise to himself that he would return his people to peace.

Even if this meant a showdown with Malful.

What Tricore did not know was that over the last two cycles, he had grown about two feet. He now stood at nine foot five, about two feet short of Malful. Most of the Takers had noticed this, and they believed they had a new leader in the making. But this leader was different; he was understanding, not like the last leaders, who were evil and would only lead for self-gain, not for their people.

But this new leader was understanding. He cared about his people.

Tricore and his people started down through the path in the swamp heading south back to where they had started from. In the distance he could see thousands of Takers gathering at the start of the blue forest. *That's odd*, he thought to himself, *I thought they were supposed to be all out searching for the strangers.* He could see Malful with twelve to fifteen Takers around him on ground that was slightly elevated. Tricore was on elevated ground as well.

Tricore asked his Takers to stay at the stream till he spoke to Malful.

He needed to sort out some issues with Malful.

The Takers remained at the stream. Their numbers were only six or seven hundred, and he knew they were no match for Malful's army.

All he wanted was permission to take his Takers back home, which he knew was going to be hard to get.

Tricore headed off to where Malful was, knowing he must be careful.

Because Malful was sneaky and sly, and he did not want to get caught by Malful or his followers. Not now when he had a chance to take some of his people back to their own lands and to live a normal life.

Grandad

The back door opened. Grandma turned around from the oven to face the back door.

"Hi, Dad." This was Grandma's name for Grandad, and he called her Nora. Why she never understood as her name was Betty. Maybe it was in the early days when he came home from work and ask what's for dinner. She would tell him, and he would say, "Ah, bloody Nora."

"Hi, Nora."

"Want some coffee?"

"Yes, please, and I need to have a chat."

"Is it about you going outside the protected lands?"

"I should have known that you would know already."

She just looked at him.

"Well, anyway, I had to help the kids. They were in a tight spot."

"Yes, I know, and you used the power of the crystals to help you change outside the lands."

Grandad started to fiddle with his thumbs. "Yes."

"And now?"

"And now there is a lot of trouble going on with the new leader of the Takers, and he must be stopped before he destroys everything."

"So what do you want to do?"

"Well, Nora, I want to use the power of the blue crystal to take my Tallis out of the lands, to help a young Taker called Tricore, who is about to go into battle with about seven hundred Takers against Malful. He has thousands of followers."

Grandma sat down and looked at Grandad. "You know that if this goes wrong, it's the end for all of us."

"And I also know if I don't do something, we will never see the kids again."

"The crystal will only work if you are doing something right. You know that, and there is a time limit on the crystal. It will only work for a short period, and I don't know how long that is."

"Yes, I do. But, Nora, it's a chance I have to take, and I will know when I get to the edge of the lands how long I have."

Grandma got up and walked over to the press. Over the sink, she opened the right side door and reached in, taking out an old shoe box. She crossed back to the table and sat down. She looked at Grandad as she opened the shoe box.

"I hope you're doing the right thing."

Putting her hand inside the shoe box, she took out a tea towel. She unwrapped the tea towel to reveal a blue crystal. It was a blue Grandad had never seen before. Grandma handed the crystal to Grandad.

"Please be careful."

"I will, Nora, I promise."

Grandad put the crystal to his forehead. The crystal lit up, sending a blue light into Grandad's head. This lasted for all two seconds. Grandad's eyes turned a very bright sky blue; Grandad handed the crystal back to Grandma.

"Thanks, Nora." Grandad got up from the table and leaned forward and kissed Grandma.

"I have to go, Nora, and time is short."

"I know, Dad, just be safe."

Grandad stepped backed from the table. He started to shake; his body started to change shape. Within seconds, he was a Tallis.

"Be a good boy, Jack, and bring the kids back home to me safe."

Jack nudged Grandma and let out a little growl.

"Thank you, and I know you will."

With that, Jack went out to the garden. Once in the garden, he let out a massive roar, a roar that was heard through all of Mogieland.

The other six Tallis came at speed to Jack. He nudged all six one at a time. As he did so, their eyes changed to blue. With the change of the color of their eyes also came the knowledge of what they had to do.

When this was done, the six Tallis set off at speed. The seventh Tallis stayed at Grandma's house; the other six Tallis headed south of Grandma's. Heading for the blue forest, Jack led, and the five Tallis followed at speed, speed that was never seen before. They had a job to do, and it meant the difference between life and death for all in Mogieland.

Malful and Tricore

Tricore came across from the stream to where Malful was with his twelve Takers. As soon as Tricore approached, they all stopped talking and looked up at Tricore. Malful was the first one to speak.

"Ah, young Tricore, you have grown a lot since I have seen you last."

"Thank you, Malful."

Malful nodded.

"You have canvassed the wise man's borders."

"Yes, Malful, I have."

"And what news do you bring me? Good news, I hope."

"Some good and some bad news, Malful."

"Okay, start with the bad news first, and then it has to get better."

"Two of our Takers were killed outside the wise man's lands by the Tallis. Well, they were killed in the manner that the Tallis kill."

Malful stood up to full height; Tricore stepped back.

"Outside the wise man's lands? This cannot be, the Tallis cannot leave their lands. You must be mistaken."

"I wish I was mistaken."

"And the good news?"

"We have found a way into the wise man's lands on the north border. But it is only big enough for one Taker at a time."

"You call this good news?"

"Yes, Malful, it's what you sent us to find, and it's what we found."

Malful's eyes narrowed.

"You only half the job I sent you to do."

Tricore rose to full height and felt the urge to strike out at Malful, but he held back for the sake of the Takers that had followed him.

Malful stood his ground.

"There must be a way into the wise man's lands that is bigger than the way you found. Take your people and go and search the borders of the wise man's lands again."

"My Takers are tired, they want to go back to our lands. They are sick of all this running around looking for strangers and getting killed in their hundreds. They want to go home to see their families."

"They can go when the strangers are caught or dead, and we have control over the wise man's lands and not before."

"I will bring this news back to them."

"Yes, you do that."

Tricore backed away from Malful. Once at a safe distance, he turned and started to walk away. When he heard a roar, he turned around and looked at Malful.

"What was that?" Malful said to the Takers that were sitting around him. They all shook their heads. Malful looked at Tricore.

"Do you know?"

Tricore told Malful that he did not know.

But the sound shook the land and sent fear throughout the Takers.

Tricore turned around and continued on his way. He decided to go to the right of his Takers and join his group from the rear. He needed time to think. Malful had not given him much of a choice, and he knew his group was waiting for him to return, to lead them home. Tricore entered into some trees. He was confused. He knew he wasn't strong enough to challenge Malful, but he wanted to lead his own people. Tricore sat down or a rock. He looked around. Nothing, only trees. Good, he needed the peace and quiet. Tricore sat and started to think of his options, which at this stage, were very limited.

Tricore was sitting with his head down looking at the ground. He felt kind of odd. All of a sudden, as if someone was watching him, Tricore looked up. Sitting about six feet away from him was a Tallis. Tricore froze. He just stared at the Tallis, and the Tallis stared at him.

Tricore knew he was about to die, and no matter what he did, he knew he would be dead in the blink of an eye. He knew of the speed of the Tallis. As he sat watching the Tallis, the Tallis started to change. Tricore just looked, the Tallis changed into a stranger.

"Tricore, we need to talk."

"Who are you, and what do you want from me?"

"I want nothing from you other than to help you."

"Why do you want to help me?"

"Not you, Tricore, but your people."

"Why would a Tallis want to help my people?"

"It's a long story, Tricore, but your people need to return to their own lands, and this will never happen under the rule of Malful. You need to rule your people, and it looks like you need all the help you can get."

Tricore went to stand up. As he did, five more Tallis came out of the trees. Tricore sat back down; the Tallis all sat beside the stranger.

"Do you want my help?"

Tricore looked at the stranger. "Yes."

"Right, so this is what we must do."

When they had finished talking, Grandad changed back to a Tallis, and the Tallis all headed back into the woods.

Tricore got up off the rock and headed back to his people.

Tricore came out of the woods at the back of his people. When they saw him coming, they moved toward him, waiting to see what was said with his meeting with Malful.

Tricore walked to the center of his people. He told them what Malful had said, and he also told them of his plans.

The Takers had nothing to lose. They did not know the part about the Tallis, and they knew they would all be killed, but it was better to die than serve under Malful.

Tricore called one of the Takers, "I need you to go to Malful and tell him that I will not follow his instructions, and that we are prepared to fight and die where we are. Now go and do this for me."

When the Taker left for Malful's camp, Tricore set about arranging his Takers on the slight hill where they were camped.

Balgus came over to Tricore.

"So we are going to stand our ground. What chance do you think we will have? I will tell you, Tricore."

"No, Balgus, I will tell you. We have a very good chance, and when this is all over, and we are back in our own lands, you will come to me and apologize to me for underestimating me."

"But, Tricore, we are only about eight or nine hundred strong, they have thousands."

"Balgus, we have much work to do and a short time to do it. So please help me or stay out of my way."

"Okay, Tricore, what do you want me to do?"

"We need to line the Takers up in a V shape with the point facing Malful's army."

"Okay, I think."

They started to arrange the Takers into the V shape.

Across the divide, Malful watched as the Takers gathered around Tricore, and as a single Taker left the group and headed toward Malful, what happened next baffled Malful.

Tricore and some other Taker started to arrange their group into a V shape. Some of the Takers that were standing beside Malful asked Malful, "What's going on?"

"I don't know, but,"—he pointed at the single Taker approaching—"I think we are going to find out."

The Taker approached Malful.

"I have a message for you from Tricore."

"And what would that message be?"

"Tricore said he would rather die where he is than serve under you."

"Oh, that's what he said."

"Yes, Malful."

"Okay, now you go back to Tricore and tell him I said if that's his choice, then so be it."

The Taker took off at speed. On his way back, he noticed that all his people were in a V shape.

Malful turned to his trusted Takers.

"Tricore wants a war, so shall we give him a war, not that it will last long.

Get your people ready, this should not take long. When your people are ready, call me. I will lead them into battle."

The Takers took off, heading back into their groups, setting them up for the forthcoming battle. They set themselves up into fourteen groups of a thousand a group. When they were ready, they informed Malful.

"Good, but we won't need all them groups, three or four should do. But keep them on standby just in case."

Malful headed down to the front of the groups. He turned and faced them. "Before you, you will see some Takers who have decided to do battle with us rather than catch and kill the strangers. These are the Takers I told you about, the ones who betrayed their own. If they want a war, then we will give them one." Malful turned and faced Tricore's men.

Tricore came out of his group. He faced Malful and his people.

"I stand here before you to give you this chance to walk away before this battle starts. There is no need for us to fight among ourselves. We can all to return home and live in our own lands."

He stood and watched for a reaction, but there was none. Tricore turned and returned to the front of the V.

Malful raised his hand. As he did, two Tallis came out of the trees and went down to the sharp point of the V, each taking up position either side of the point. When they stopped, two more Tallis came out of the trees and took up a position behind the first two. The Takers in the V could not believe their eyes. Then two more Tallis came out of the trees, taking up their position behind the others. When the last two Tallis stopped, the ground on each side of the Tallis and to the front of them started to move. In seconds there were twelve Vox positioned in a line across the Tallis.

Malful was still standing with his hand in the air.

Click, click. From behind Tricore's V came a swarm of Clickers, they stopped in midair and hovered above Tricore's men. There were about a thousand Clickers. There was a loud clicking noise that was louder than the swarm of Clickers. When Tricore looked up, he saw a Clicker, unlike anything he has seen before. It was about twenty to twenty-five feet long Tricore said to himself, *This must be their leader.* Tricore could hear the talking among the Takers. They now had hope; they could not believe that there was so much help there for them.

Malful slowly lowered his hand, looking across the clearing. He knew he had no hope of winning the battle. He knew if this battle started, that the Clickers and the Vox would wipe out every Taker behind him, and what was worse was every Taker behind him knew the same.

He also knew that if he called charge, he would be the only one to go forward because there was not one Taker that would follow him.

Tricore again walked out from his position down toward Malful.

"Again, I will give you this last chance to walk away. If you do, no harm will come to you. But there are conditions, and the conditions are as follows: One, you must return to our lands, the land of the Takers; two, you must hand over Malful and his trusted Takers to the wise man; three, you must never leave our lands again unless you have special permission from the wise man. I will give you some time to think about this." Tricore turned and rejoined his people.

After only a few minutes, hundreds of Malful's Takers left the ranks and headed toward their own lands, but a lot stayed.

Malful looked back at his people. He was losing about a third. Now his chances were getting small. With nothing to lose, Malful raised his hand again and roared, "Charge!"

Malful ran forward, and only about four or five hundred Takers followed him. Tricore and his people did not need to move. The Clicker leader and his Clickers took off and swooped down on Malful and his men. The lead Clicker, who was the leader, went straight for Malful. Malful was the first to be picked off. The rest of the Takers were gone in seconds, and when the Clickers were gone, all that was left were the Takers that did not charge, the ones that had left the ranks.

Tricore walked over to Jack.

"I don't know how you did all this in such short a time, but I wish to say thank you."

Jack just let out a small growl. He looked around, and then he let out a roar. The Vox disappeared back into the ground, and Jack took off with his Tallis, back to the wise man's lands and home.

Sarah and the Fifth Thorn

"Sarah, how much farther is it to the fifth thorn? I mean to the place that we have to put the thorn in?"

"I don't know, Steven."

"Well, we seemed to be travelling for ages and getting nowhere fast."

"Don't you think I know that?"

"Yes, I know you do, but you must have some idea on how far it is."

"Steven, I know what you know, nothing more and nothing less."

"Hay, you two, what are we looking for?"

"The elder oak, Louis, I told you that already."

"Well, duh."

Sarah turned around facing Louis. Louis was standing pointing up into the air.

Sarah looked up. The tree went up toward the sky, and it went on forever.

"Is that it?"

"You know, Louis, you might just be right."

"Well, what do we do now?"

"Hang on a second." Sarah reached into her bag. "No, not that one or that one. Yes, this one."

Steven and Louis were looking on in amazement.

Sarah took out a crystal from her bag.

"I think you might need this as well." Steven handed over a funny-shaped crystal to Sarah.

Sarah took the crystal from Steven. Holding it beside her own crystal, she found that the two crystals fitted together. Once together, they started to shine. Sarah put the crystals at the base of the tree.

"Look at the size of that tree. It must be thirty feet wide. I hope the crystals are in the right place."

"I don't know, Steven, I think we will just have to wait and see."

"But what if the opening is on the other side? We will never see it."

"Right then, Louis, that's a good point. You go around the other side and watch for the opening."

"Okay, Sarah, no problem."

"And, Steven, will you watch that side?"

"Sure will, Sarah."

Louis had gone around the other side of the tree. He sat on the ground watching the base of the tree.

Louis looked up. He could not see Sarah or Steven.

"Hay, are you still there?"

"Yes, Louis, we are still here. Are you all right?"

"Sure thing, Sarah, I was never better."

"Good then, if you see anything, call me."

Steven was sitting, watching the base of the tree. He could see Sarah, and Sarah could see him.

"Are you all right, Steven?"

"Yes, sure."

Louis was sitting crossed-legged, facing the tree. He did not hear the Taker come up behind him till it was too late. He felt the claw go over his mouth. In seconds, he felt tired, and then he passed out.

"Hay, Louis, have you any of that chocolate left?"

There was no answer.

"Louis, have you fallen asleep again?"

Still no answer.

Steven got up and went around the tree. As he did, he saw Louis stretched out. Steven stopped.

"That's not right. Louis is black."

Steven put his hand into his bag and grabbed hold of the salt. Taking the salt out of the bag, he opened it. Steven moved slowly around the tree, then he saw him, a Taker. He was sitting two feet away from Louis. Steven stepped out in front of the Taker. The Taker was up on his feet in a flash, and he went straight for Steven. Steven sidestepped the Taker. As the Taker passed him, Steven emptied the bag of salt over him. The Taker screamed. In a second, blood started to come out of the Taker through little holes where the salt had landed. The Taker ran into the trees screaming.

Steven ran over to Louis. He dropped to his knees beside his brother. Sarah was on her knees beside Steven.

"Is he all right, Steven?"

"I don't know. He's very cold and look at his skin, it's black."

Steven put his head down on Louis's chest.

"I can't hear his heart."

Sarah put her ear to Louis's mouth.

"Steven, I can't feel any breath."

"No, this can't be happening." Steven shook Louis.

"Wake up, Louis, wake up. Come on, please."

Sarah started crying. "Come, Louis, it's time to go home please, please."

Louis did not move; he just lay there.

Sarah looked at Steven; Steven started crying.

"Sarah, what are we going to do?"

Sarah looked at Steven and just shook her head. "I don't know."

Behind them, the bark of the tree started to open. Both Steven and Sarah turned around and looked.

"Sarah, you have to do what you're meant to do."

Sarah looked at Steven.

"It all seems pointless now."

"I know, but you have to do it."

Sarah nodded. She got up of her knees and went over to the tree where the bark had opened. It was only a small opening. Sarah could not see into it. Sarah reached up to her hair and removed the hairpin. Looking at the hairpin, she just said, "Stephanie." And she placed the hairpin into the hole. As soon as she did, the hole in the bark closed. Sarah got back up and went back over to Steven.

Steven was holding Louis and still crying. Sarah put her arms around both Steven and Louis, and she started crying.

"Sarah, we have to get Louis back to Nan's, and we have to do it quick."

Steven got Louis up on to his shoulders and started back the way they had come, heading for the wise man's house,

Sarah walked behind Steven. She felt useless. There was nothing she could do but walk and watch. They were not getting anywhere fast.

Sarah noticed the sky was getting brighter.

"That's odd."

Steven carried Louis for about an hour, then he had to stop.

"I have to stop for a few minutes to catch my breath. We could do with some help."

Steven put Louis down and fell down beside him.

Sarah said nothing; there was nothing she could say. She put her hand on Louis's face. He was still the same.

Sarah took out the whistle from her bag. She looked at it, remembering what Grandma had said.

"If you're in trouble, blow on the whistle."

"When will I know, Nana?"

"You will know."

Sarah put the whistle to her lips and blew. She then put the whistle back into her bag. She did not know if it had worked, and if it did, what help she was going to get, if any at all, and when.

"Right, it's time to go." Steven lifted Louis back up on to his shoulders and started off again. They had only travelled about thirty feet when they heard noises coming from the trees in front of them. They both stopped. "Did you hear that, Sarah?"

"Yes, I did."

From out of the trees came a giant Taker. He was maybe eleven feet tall.

Sarah and Steven froze.

The Taker looked at the two of them then at Louis.

"What's wrong with him?"

"One of your Takers drained his life."

"And you are?"

"I am his brother, Steven."

"Well, Steven, why don't you put your brother down, and I will look at him and see if I can help."

"No, and don't you put one finger near him."

"I don't think you understand, I only want to help."

"Why would you want to help us?"

"Look, Steven, time is not on your side. Do you want me to help you?"

Steven looked at Sarah and then back at the Taker.

"No, I don't want your help, not now not ever."

"Steven, I think that any help we can get for Louis we should take."

"I don't want him or his kind touching my brother."

"But he might be able to help us."

Steven looked at Sarah. Deep down he knew she was right.

"But how can we trust him?"

"Steven, if he was going to attack us, he would have done it by now."

Steven put Louis down on the ground.

The Taker walked over to where Louis lay. He got down on his knees and put both his hands on Louis's chest.

"This is not good."

"Is he dead?"

"No, Steven, he is not. But if we don't get him help very soon, he will be."

"But where can we get help out here in the middle of nowhere?"

"I don't know."

"Can you help? Can you carry him back to the wise man's?"

"I am sorry, but who are you?"

"I am Sarah."

"Well, Sarah, you are the one with the thorn, and you have replaced it, is that right?"

"Yes, it is, but how did you know?"

"Because the spell is back in place. We, I mean the Takers, can only move to the north. The spell stops us from going south. This is the way the spell works. It forces us back to our own lands. So if I wanted to, I cannot help you. The only thing I can do is tell you what you must do. I will return some life back to him, it will give you some extra time but not much."

The Taker put his hands back on Louis's chest. After about two minutes, he took away his hands.

"I don't know if that will help you, but it's all I can do for him."

"I think it will give us all the time we need."

The Taker and the kids turned around only to see Grandad standing a few feet away from them.

"Grandad, Louis was attacked by one of them."

"I know, Steven, but all Takers are not the same."

The Taker got up and walked over to Grandad.

"I am sorry, but I have done all I can."

"And for that, I thank you, Tricore."

"It is nothing when you think of all you have done for me."

"Let's just say we are even." They both shook hands.

"Now, Tricore, you are going to visit the wise man's lands."

"But how can this be?"

"Trust me, it is possible."

"I trust you, my friend."

Tricore went back to where Louis lay and picked him up.

"Okay, I am ready."

"Okay, we need to get to the clearing at the edge of the woods. It is not too far, then there will be help there waiting for us."

"What help, Grandad?"

"Wait and see, Steven."

They started off for the forest's edge.

They travelled very fast.

Sarah and Steven were finding it hard to keep up with Tricore and Grandad. After a while, they came to the forest edge. Just beyond the trees, they could see Annie. She was standing, waiting. As soon as they got near Annie, a pink haze started to form around Annie. She called for them to hurry.

Tricore was first to get to Annie then Grandad. Sarah and Steven arrived together. The haze covered all six of them. It started to get very thick. No one could see out through it, and it changed from pink to green then to blue, then it started to clear. When it cleared, they were all standing outside the wise man's house, and the six Tallis were lying in the grass off to the right.

"Okay, Tricore, you can give him to me now. I think you're too big to go through the door."

Tricore gently took Louis off his shoulders and handed him to Grandad. Grandad went straight into the house. As he went in the door of the house, Grandma was waiting.

"Put him on the bed, Dad." Grandad did as he was asked. Steven and Sarah came in the door.

"Can we help, Nana?"

"No, thank you, Sarah. You have done all you can for now, it's up to us from here on in."

Steven and Sarah went over to the table and sat there. Nana went to a press over by the back door. She opened the press.

"Now where did I put it?"

Rooting around the press, she found what she was looking for. It looked like a bag of marbles. She crossed the room to Louis and placed the bag on his chest.

"That's all we can do for now. We just have to wait now and be patient. I think we could all do with a nice cup of tea and some apple tart."

Sarah started crying.

"That's all Louis wanted, Nana, just some apple tart."

"I know, Sarah bear, but sometimes you have to go with the flow."

"Let's leave him to rest, and we will go out to the garden. You can tell me everything that happened to you, and we can all have something to drink and eat while we are waiting."

"How long, Nana?"

"How long what, Sarah?"

"How long have we to wait for Louis to get better?"

"I don't know, Sarah bear, could be minutes, could be hours."

"But he is going to get better, Nana."

"Yes, Sarah bear, he is. But it will take time like everything else."

"Okay, Nana."

Sarah turned to Steven and shrugged her shoulders.

Steven did not say anything. They both left the house and went out to the gardens together.

"Looks like it's time to wait, Sarah."

"Yes, Steven, it looks like that."

The Garden

Nana, Sarah, and Steven went out to the garden and crossed over to the table. They sat down beside Angela. Angela was sitting at the picnic table with Grandad and Tricore. Tricore was a little uneasy as four of the Tallis were sitting, watching Tricore. Angela noticed this and said it to Grandad.

"I am sorry you feel uncomfortable, Tricore. I will get the Tallis to move back up the garden a bit."

"Thank you."

Grandad turned to the Tallis, but before he could say anything, the Tallis took off at speed, heading in the direction of the black forest.

Grandad excused himself and left.

"My, something's amiss."

"Yes, Annie, something is wrong."

"Do you know what it is, Nana?"

"No, Sarah bear, I don't."

"I do," said Tricore, "there are Takers at the north barrier."

"How do you know that?"

"Well, young"—Tricore thought for a second—"Sarah bear, I can smell them."

Everybody laughed.

"Did I say something wrong?"

"No, mister Tricore, it's just, well, my name is Sarah, and Nana, I mean, the wise man calls me Sarah bear."

"Oh, I am sorry, Sarah."

"It's okay. TAZMAZ!" Sarah jumped up from the seat and ran toward Tazmaz. He was walking with Grandad and four of the Tallis. Sarah wrapped her arms around Tazmaz's waist; Tazmaz bent down and gave Sarah a hug.

"Who is that, Nana?"

"That, Steven, is Tazmaz, the leader of the Earth Keepers."

"Come on, Tazmaz, come and sit with us."

"Tazmaz, this is Annie, the gatekeeper. And this is Nana, the wise man. This is Steven, my cousin, and this is Tricore."

"I am happy to meet you all."

"Tricore I have never heard of you."

"I am the new leader of the Takers."

"Well, Tricore, I am happy to meet you."

Before other words were spoken, there was a loud *click, click*. Everybody looked up at the sky to see a very large Clicker coming in and hovering just feet away, then he landed.

"My, we have a lot of visitors," said Nana.

"Yes, we have, and there is more to come," said Grandad.

"More to come, Dad? Did you invite all of Mogieland for tea?"

"Not all." Grandad got up from the table and went into the house. Once inside the house he crossed over to the bed to where Louis was. Grandad sat on the edge of the bed.

"Well, mister, you got yourself into a mess this time." Grandad looked at the crystals; they were not much brighter. Grandad rubbed Louis's face. "Hang in there, mister." Grandad kissed his forehead and then got up from the bed and went back out of the house and back over to the picnic table.

"How is the little Louis?"

"Still the same, Tricore."

"You might think this is odd, but I have an idea that might help."

"Anything that helps is a bonus. What's your idea?"

"If I can draw some energy from somewhere, I might be able to transfer it back to the little one."

"Okay, it's worth a try. What do you need?"

"Well, caretaker"—Tricore looked around—"that," he said, pointing to a large apple tree in the center of the garden.

Grandad's face frowned. That apple tree was his pride and joy.

"Well, I suppose if that's what you need then so be it."

Tricore got up from the table and walked over to the tree. When he got to the tree, he placed both hands on the bark.

Tazmaz, Steven, Sarah, Angela, Nana, Grandad, and the Clicker watched as the tree went from a healthy green to a light shade of gray then to a dark shade of gray then to black. Once the tree was black, Tricore removed his hands from the tree, turning to face everybody.

"I think that was plenty."

Tricore crossed over to Grandad.

"Now I have to go to the little one." Grandad led the way; everyone else followed. Grandad was first to go into the house, then with a lot of difficulty, Tricore got through the doorway, followed by the rest, except the Clicker. He was far too big to get through the door. Tricore bent over and made his way to the bed where Louis was lying. Tricore got down on his knees beside the bed and placed his hands on Louis's chest. Everybody was watching. After seconds, Sarah said, "Look, the crystals are getting brighter."

Everyone looked; the crystals were getting brighter. Tricore took his hand away, looking at Nana. "That's all I can do for him. It's up to the little one now."

"Thank you for what you have done."

Tricore got up off his knees and went back across the room, bent over and somehow managed to get through the door. They all followed, except

Nana. She sat on the edge of the bed looking at Louis and the bag on his chest. Nana held Louis's hand and put her hand on Louis's face.

"Come on, Louis, show them what you're made of. You're a fighter, and I have a special job for you." Nana bent over Louis and kissed his forehead. "You show them."

At the table sat Grandad, Sarah, and Tricore. Facing them was Steven, Tazmaz, and Angela. The Clicker was standing at the end of the table.

Grandad passed around a small bottle.

"I need all of you to take a small drink from this bottle."

"Why, Grandad?"

"It will help us all to understand each other."

The bottle was passed around, and everyone took a small sip.

Nana sat at the end of the table beside Grandad.

"Now that that's done, we can get on with why we are all here, for this I will pass you over to the wise man."

"Thank you, Grandad.

"Well, first of all, I want to clear up some things. The fifth thorn was not taken from Mogieland by Stephanie. Well, it was, but she did not know what it was. It was given to her by the leader of the Takers, and he knew what trouble it would cause. If the thorn left these lands, and it would also give him the chance to gain power. As we all know, this is what happened. But now the thorn has been replaced, the skies are no longer black, they are returning to their normal colors, and the Takers are, as we know, they are returning to their own lands. This is thanks to Tricore. Things will return to normal over a short period. But there will be some changes that will take place here in Mogieland. The first is, no one will be allowed to enter anyone else's lands without permission from the leader of that land and the approval from the wise man. Each leader will be allowed to rule his lands as he sees fit.

"Second is, each leader will be allowed to enter my lands, with my permission for social or official reasons. Each leader must travel on to my lands alone. Otherwise, the Tallis will, and I mean, will destroy any other persons travelling with their leader, so be warned about this, there will be no exceptions.

"Third is, over the next twelve full moons, power will be changed from the wise man, me, to Sarah and from the caretaker, Grandad, to Steven and last of all, from the gate keeper, Angela, to Louis."

"It's always the same, talking about me as if I am not even here."

Everybody turned around to see Louis standing outside the front door of the house.

"Is there any apple and fruit tart left?"

Sarah was first to run. She jumped up of the seat and ran to Louis, wrapping both arms around his neck.

"Hay, you gave us a bad scare. We all thought you were dead. Are you all right?"

"Yes, I am, but I am hungry."

"Well, it seems there is nothing wrong with you," she said as she gave him a big hug.

Steven was right behind Sarah. He wrapped his arms around Louis.

Nana, Grandad, and Angela all wrapped their arms around Louis.

"Hay, what's all the fuss about? All I want is some apple and fruit pie."

Everyone laughed.

Grandad looked at Tricore. "Thank you."

"You're more than welcome. I was not sure if it would work."

"Nana, can I ask you a question?"

"Yes, Louis."

"Why is it every time I come here, I wake up in your bed?"

"That's a long story, Louis, and it will have to wait till later."

"Oh okay, but, Nana, I am really hungry. Can I have some pie?"

"Okay, you go and sit beside Sarah, and I will bring some pie to you."

Louis went over and sat beside Sarah, and Nana went into the house.

After a short while, Nana arrived back at the table. She brought out a large plate with twelve slices of pie on it. She placed the plate on the center of the table, and then she sat down.

"Are they all for me?"

"No, Louis, they are for everybody."

"Ah, sh—"

"Louis."

"Sorry, Annie."

"I will continue with what I was saying. Fourth is, any person who enters another person's lands without permission will have to deal with the Tallis. From today, I will be granting the power to the Tallis to leave the wise man's land on the wise man's instruction only. They will stop trouble before it starts. We don't want things to get as bad as this again.

"Fifth is, there will be a meeting here every third full moon with the wise man and all the leaders of the lands. This meeting will be held to sort out any issues that have arisen, and last of all, I wish to thank you all for the help you gave to me and mine during these troubles."

Nana noticed that everybody was eating pie, except Tricore.

"Tricore, why are you not eating?"

"I am sorry, wise man, I don't mean to offend, but I don't know how to eat. It has been a long time since we done that."

"Okay then, I suppose it's time you started to learn."

Nana took up a slice of pie and handed it to Tricore; she then took a slice of pie for herself.

"Now, Tricore, watch what I do."

Nana put the pie into her mouth and bit. She then started to chew.

Tricore put the pie into his mouth and bit; he also started to chew.

Nana swallowed. Tricore tried to swallow but was finding it hard to do. He was even finding it hard to chew.

"Try and relax, it will help."

Louis went over to Tricore and stood in front of him. Don't think about it. Otherwise, you will never swallow. It's like eating sprouts, just chew and swallow."

Louis looked over at the forest.

"Hay, why are there a lot of Takers coming over here?"

Everybody looked.

"Where?"

"Nowhere, I was only joking." Louis looked back at Tricore.

"See, it's gone because you did not think about it."

Tricore smiled. "You are a very clever young man."

"Ouch, trying to swallow that it must have been sore."

"Louis, don't be rude."

"Sorry, Annie." He muttered "witch" under his breath.

"No, it's okay," said Tricore, and he took another bite of the pie. "I can get use to this, it's good."

Tazmaz stood up.

"Thank you for everything, but I think it's time I went back to my lands. If there is nothing else, that I should know."

"No, Tazmaz, that's about it all till our next meeting."

"Thank you, wise man, see you all soon."

Sarah stood up and went over to Tazmaz.

"I am sorry about Taz. There was nothing I could do."

"It's okay, Sarah, I was told everything, even the way you saved Wapz, and it's I who should be thanking you for all you have done for me and my people. Well, I best be going. I have been gone far too long from my lands." Tazmaz said good-bye to everybody.

Everybody said good-bye. Tazmaz left. Behind him walked two of the Tallis. They followed him to the edge of the wise man's lands.

"It's time I went also."

Everybody looked around; it was the Clicker that spoke.

Steven's mouth fell open. "You can talk."

"Yes, I can."

"So why didn't you talk before now?"

"I had nothing to say."

"Well, I suppose that's as good an answer as any."

"Thank you, my friend, for coming."

"Thank you, caretaker, if you need my help again, you know where you will find me."

"I will, and again, thank you."

With that, the Clicker took off into the air and was gone in seconds.

Everybody turned to see Tricore still eating. Tricore looked up.

"Oh, I am sorry, but this is nice."

"Told you, Nana, it's the best pie in the world."

"Thank you, Louis. Tricore, I will give you some for your trip home."

"Thank you." Tricore stood up. He walked over to Grandad. "And thank you for everything you have done for me. Without you and your friends, we all would be out there under the rule of Malful, and I am sure that most of my people will agree with me. He was one leader we would rather not have."

Nana headed back into the house.

"You're welcome, Tricore, and remember you now have the Tallis to help you if you need."

"Yes, I will remember." Tricore held out his hand.

Grandad put out his hand; they both shook hands.

Nana returned with a small picnic basket. In it were four apple and fruit pies.

"Here you are, Tricore, something for your trip."

"Thank you."

"You are welcome, and remember, it will take some time to get used to eating again. But take it slow, and it will all fall back into place. I have also arranged for the Clickers to drop off some fruits into your lands as often as they can, and as soon as I can, I will arrange for some of the Earth Keepers to go to your lands and help you to start growing food again."

"Thank you again, caretaker."

"You are welcome anytime, my friend."

Tricore turned and headed off across the wise man's lands with two Tallis walking behind him, happy now that he had made some friends and not enemies and that he could also eat.

"I am glad for that because those pies sure taste nice."

Nana, Grandad, and Annie went back to the table and sat down.

"Well, I think it's time, Dad."

"Yes, I think it is, Nora."

Nana called the kids to the table.

The kids all sat down at the table.

"What's wrong, Nana?"

"Nothing, but it's time for us to go back to our own time and land."

"Louis, you look so sad. What's wrong?"

"You gave Tricore all the pies."

"Don't you worry, Louis, there's plenty more in the kitchen. Now that we are all sitting here, are we ready to go?"

Everybody answered yes.

"Okay, Annie, it's your turn."

Annie took two crystals from a pouch and held them out in front of her in one hand. The crystals started to glow. A pink mist formed around the table. The mist went thicker and thicker, then the mist changed to blue and red. It was nice in the mist; it was quiet and peaceful. The mist started to clear. When it did, they were all sitting at the picnic table in Grandma's back garden.

"Well, we are home. Time for dinner."

"Nana, what day is it?"

"Sunday, of course, Sarah."

Sarah looked at her watch. It was three forty-five.

"Is it Sunday afternoon, Nana?"

"Yes, Sarah, time moves a lot faster in Mogieland than it does here. We have only been gone a few hours."

"Only a few hours? That's hard to believe."

"Try telling someone where you have been. Now that's hard."

"Okay, it's time for dinner, and tomorrow, you will all start your training in your new roles as caretaker, gatekeeper, and wise man. But for now, I think you should all go and have a shower and get changed. You all look a right mess."

Sarah and Steven got up from the table and headed toward the house, but Louis stayed sitting at the table.

Nana looked at Louis.

"Is there something wrong?"

"No, Nana."

"Then why are you not going for your shower?"

"Oh, now?"

"Yes, now."

"Well, when we were back in monkey land, you said you had more pies."

"Louis, go and have your shower, then after dinner, you can have some pie."

"Ah, Nana."

"Go, Louis, and tell Sarah not to forget to ring home after her shower."

"Okay, Nana."

Louis got up from the table and headed toward the house.

"He's a handful."

"Yes, Annie, he is. But his heart is in the right place."

"Yes, that's for sure, and he almost gave up his life for something he believed in."

"Yes, he is like the other two fighters."

"What's wrong with you, Grandad?"

"I am just wondering, Annie, how I am going to get my apple tree back to life."

"Don't worry, Grandad, I will help you sort it out."

"Thanks, Annie."

"Talking about sorting things out, I suppose I better get some dinner started," Nana said as she was getting up from the table.

"And I will help you."

"Thanks, Annie."

"And I will collect some apples. You're going to need a lot over the next few weeks now that Louis is staying. I hope there's enough trees in the gardens."

Nana and Annie both laughed together.

"I wasn't being funny. That lad can eat apple and fruit pies till the cows come home, I just wonder where he puts it all."

"He's a growing lad."

"Yes, he is, and at the rate he eats pies, he will be as big as Tricore."

Nana laughed. "Right, I am going to put on the dinner. You lot can head up and have a shower before dinner's ready."

"And, Louis, keep out of the river."

"That's not funny, Nana."

The kids headed to their rooms. Grandad headed out to the garden to look after his apple trees, and Annie went to gather the crystals that they would need to start the kids' training tomorrow. This is one thing she would not like, giving over her powers to the kids; but it had to be done, and it would take most of, if not all of, the four weeks that the kids would be staying. Annie looked back at the gardens, and she started to laugh. Grandad was jumping up and down, shouting at the crows, and she swears she could hear the crows laughing at Grandad.

The end

Lightning Source UK Ltd.
Milton Keynes UK
18 January 2011

165891UK00001B/43/P